Titles by L

Dogs in the Sun

G. D. Nyamndi

Langaa Research & Publishing CIG
Mankon, Bamenda

Publisher:
Langaa RPCIG
Langaa Research & Publishing Common Initiative Group
P.O. Box 902 Mankon
Bamenda
North West Region
Cameroon
Langaagrp@gmail.com
www.langaa-rpcig.net

Distributed outside N. America by African Books Collective
orders@africanbookscollective.com
www.africanbookscollective.com

Distributed in N. America by Michigan State University Press
msupress@msu.edu
www.msupress.msu.edu

ISBN: 9956-558-58-3

DISCLAIMER

The names, characters, places and incidents in this book are either the product of the author's imagination or are used fictitiously. Accordingly, any resemblance to actual persons, living or dead, events, or locales is entirely one of incredible coincidence.

Contents

Chapter One

My name is Banda. Banda son of Gakoh, of Nwemba.

Nwembwana founded Nwemba many many moons ago. It is said that back in the ancestral lands of Bengeta, somewhere in the deep past, he discovered himself in a feud with Ilembea, his half-brother, and paid for his lack of restraint with expulsion from the village. But that is another drink altogether...we will not whip our cowhorns dry for afofo only to be poured kwatcha.

When you hear of Nwemba you may think of it as a place where things happen that shake even the wind passing; where your morning is greeted with news that such and such has done something out of the ordinary; after all, we are talking about a village founded by Nwembwana. One would expect such a village to wear the name of its founding patriarch the way a man's frame wears his breath.

In his day you did not touch Nwembwana and get away with it. Even before Ilembea came to taste the power of his muscles, other young men of the ancestral land had eaten the dust in his hands and learnt that Nwembwana was not to be joked with. How could you defy him and still stand to tell the story? How? "Not me," he was known to say, "not my ways. I don't touch you first. Not even first. I don't touch you. But if you touch me, then stand firm." This rugged principle had borne him through life like bamboo-light through the dark.

In the fight with Ilembea, it was not Nwembwana who touched Ilembea first. When Ilembea came at him the first time he warned him off sternly: "Don't dare it a second time." But the unheeding Ilembea dared it again. And the keg caught fire.

Today, nothing of the sort. Nwemba is just a small village, timid in its aspects. If you know the way a little child with a running nose whimpers, then you have good knowledge of what I am talking about. Just imagine such a child… imagine him pulling from behind at the frill edges of his mother's cloth and refusing to trot ahead. He does not take the lead, self-made bow and arrow at the ready, filling his following mother with a proud sense of security. Frightened stiff of the path ahead, he wants to be carried, in spite of his big age. He belongs among those children who grow up because they are born and – with some chance – fed; not among those other children who impose themselves as an inescapable reality because nourished through life by courage and curiosity.

Without curiosity, without eagerness, you cannot venture far, much less face up to uncertainty when it surfaces on your path. Curiosity, eagerness, a certain desire to march out to the world and on it rather than be confined by it, a strong refusal to allow yourself to be cocooned off to some insignificant fringe: these are the muscles of a temper that enables you to see small things in big ways and big things in even bigger ways.

Nwemba does not provide any such muscles. Its own temper is soft like mud, not hard like a stone on which you can stand and see the top of the following hill; and seeing it, march on it to take possession or then to challenge its possessors.

If Nwemba were food you would compare it to foofoo. Not even the steaming type that slides deliciously down smoothened away by egusi soup with a touch of ogbono

2

and just a smattering of pepper that keeps watch over your taste buds. No, not that kind. Rather, it would be that other kind that sticks in the hand and refuses to climb to the mouth…sticks to the hand because it is half cooked, half raw…sticks because it is stranded in transformation, not knowing whether it is meant to kill the hunger in you or instead to swell the dump heap behind the house.

The village is coiled up on itself, bogged, shackled, by its own rhythm, and is content to celebrate from season to season its humdrum commonplaces, content also to see the sun when it rises, and the night each time it falls.

Day after day Nwemba rises with the waking sun and withdraws as the big red ball dips beyond the hills of Meamba. Never, not once, has a question burnt its lips about the comings and goings of the sun, or of the day, for that matter. The cyclical ritual, profound and worrying elsewhere, is to Nwemba no different from the plantain bunch you harvest behind the house, the cutting grass that strays into your forked trap in the ground, the smoke that seeps through the roof of your woman's hut.

The sleeping village lies by a river, big and deep, whose waters rush down in certain places, and in certain other places stroll like a man and his cowhorn going for an evening drink. The waters stroll down for a distance, not very long, just like from here to there, then they break into great speed, dizzying, and hit the banks in high waves, like the strolling man and his cowhorn returning from an evening of palmwine. They hit the bank like that and then crash down a deep valley and hit the floor down below in noise that even your biggest voice cannot silence. If I stand by you where those waters fall, so that you can touch me and even press my toes, if I stand by you like that, you can shout and I see the veins standing on your neck, I will not hear what you are saying, only the noise of the waters as they surge and tumble in vast, magnificent pours.

3

Another thing, as the waters fall like that they come back up again, not the same as they went down; this time they return in fine white sheets no different from cornflour that falls from a good woman's stone.

Stand by the river in this place where its waters do their return journey and it will not be long before your head enters into the sitting place of the aged ones. Place of age, place of wisdom. The waters rising back infuse the air all around with wisdom – wisdom that refreshes, wisdom that instructs. Where does it go in Nwemba?

The river is called Mantum, the soft-bellied one.

Once every year, the young men of Nwemba throw themselves in the river in a fishing contest. They swing their nets over their heads, then sink them into the river's bed and wait for what the soft belly will put in them.

The old men don't come. They remain behind in their huts and catch their pipes, heavy with nkwandang, between what are left of teeth, or then between their bare gums for most of them. Then their slack lips chew out narratives of old.

But the young girls, they come. They are the fire under the pot, the kolanut for the wine. Without them the contest will not shine; even the nets will frown – maybe even refuse to fall. They come and line the Nwemba side of the bank, ready with their wililis and their trained feet to stamp the ground and their bangled arms to wade the air. They come, many of them, ready to send their bellies into the soft belly of the river with the young men, ready also to hold their bellies in anticipation when the young men emerge heavy with fish.

When the contest comes and goes, the young men idle by the bank to hear the spirits converse and at times laugh, at certain times too even sigh.

The spirits never cry. No-one has ever heard them cry. When the talk becomes bad, they sigh, then the young men hold their ears and run away shouting no me o! no me o!

The sighs don't run after them, unless the urgency is established, in which case the fleeing young men are quickly overtaken and the sighs speed into the village to seek out the aged ones, appointed custodians of Nwemba's destiny, messengers of the will.

As the contest begins to show its head, nets appear in front of every house, and young men go from house to house comparing them to guess the winner from what they see.

The nets are of sisal beaten and spun into fibres by the women's group under Ma-Lenghi, Sendelenghi's mother, on flat-topped teak blocks collected in one place behind her house; and the spinning in front, where the women sit on the bare earth and work the mass of beaten sisal into fine threads which the men now weave into nets.

The spinning is done in silence. Ma-Lenghi sees to that ever since Chief Ndelu put the matter in her hands, told her to ensure that the session did not change into a palaver meeting where women discussed their men and – unthinkable thing – even criticized them. He'd had to do that because one of his own women had returned once from her spinning session and kept him awake all night – it was her turn in the royal bed –, denied him sleep, not the way a woman will replace sleep all night. He'd turned this way and she'd talked. Threatened with the rage of starved anger, still she'd talked. And in the morning he'd sent for Ma-Lenghi, first thing, and had sat tapping his irate feet on the ground and whistling to himself. She'd come panting and holding her chest and had bowed into the royal presence, ushered in by attendants.

"Ma-Lenghi!"

"Tchaabe!"

"Is it your men you spin or the beaten sisal?"

"Tchaabe, the beaten sisal."

"That's not what my woman tells me at night."

"Tchaabe, I'm on my knees."

5

"And you'll stay on them. Who tells you women that you decide where a man's daughter marries?" He'd asked this question half raised on his royal stool as if carried up by the surge of the affront in him.

"Tchaabe, may bad thoughts be carried away by Mantum."

"May bad thoughts be carried away by Mantum. But you women of this village have kept bad thoughts in your heads. If not, how can my own woman starve me with talk of my daughter not marrying as second wife? How can she?"

"Tchaabe, the gods of Mantum forbid."

"The gods will forbid. And you women will desist. A man sends his daughter into marriage. It has always been like that; and it will continue to be like that. And tell all the women with you: nights are for their husbands, not for kpa kpak kpa kpak."

"Tchaabe." And she had bowed out, warned and instructed.

Since this day, silence had become the only noise at the beating sessions. If a woman's mouth got tired not saying anything, she was allowed to break into song. But not just any kind of song. Songs like the one about the woman who turned her back on her man at night, songs laughing at the man who could not look at his woman in the morning – such songs were thrown out as bad. Ma-Lenghi saw to it that they went straight back to where they came from; that they never made a home in any woman's head.

But the men, they weave in song and laughter, stopping every now and again to say this or that thing about the women they have left at home, as if it was the women they were weaving and not sisal thread. They know what transpired in their Chief's night and all of them turn the story of that sleepless night this side and that looking for where to hold it and throw it far away into the bush.

6

Once Abua left the weaving and beat the air in a solemn gesture of defiance, and then let go: "The woman who will deny me my night is not yet born." To which Ntianop who always sat by him added:

"I cut three broomsticks and put in my woman's hands."

"To mean?" Fofang weaving a little way off demanded.

"My children, my food, my nights," Ntianop returned.

"I did not cut any broomsticks," Abua then said, "but Weteba knows that her life by me is three sticks in one."

"You people talk about broomsticks and nights," Fofang said without taking his eyes off his weaving. "Broomsticks, yes. And the days, what do you do with them? My days. That's where my die is. All my five children are rewards of my days."

"That's why you cut short your weaving every other time," Abua observed.

"You say it like a joke, but that's when I plant the seeds. I follow her to the farm, then we return home. After that I just water the seeds."

"I let my woman do one thing at a time." Abua said, with unusual sympathy. "What I don't take from her is telling me what to do with the children she gives me. Her duty is to give them to me. What I do with them does not concern her."

"But who ever told them that they could look into the things we do with our children?" Fofang challenged.

"Go and ask Chief Ndelu's wife," Ntianop offered. "The one who told him her girl will not be sold in second place."

"If I want I will sell my child in twentieth place," Abua said almost crowing, and sending the other weavers into prolonged fits of laughter.

"Where do these women put their heads when they sleep?" Ntianop checked his own laughter to ask.

When they were not talking about the women, it was about the coming contest, how it would change things in the village if it turned out this way, or would not if it turned out that other way.

Since my father and Winjala the Crude returned from Meamba, Nwemba had stood permanently in the crossfire of whether it was good or bad for the white man's ways to enter the village.

Not many villagers had travelled to Meamba; but the few of them who had, like Uncle Abua, often said they saw things in that place that they would like to see in their own village as well.

Ntianop for one had never left Nwemba, but he did not put away the good things that he heard about the white man from those who had seen him and his deeds in Meamba. So he asked why Winjala the Crude was so resolute on blocking the good winds: "What is his own to hold out his hands and stop the white man's things from coming to us? What is his own in this kind of way, wanting to stop Mantum from running down in its journey of many moons? Think of the water, its size, its speed…think of all that and then see Winjala, tiny Winjala, standing in the middle of the vast river and putting out his little hands and saying no don't flow again because I don't want you to flow. How do you think you can do a thing like that? I've never been to Meamba to see how the white man does his own things there, but do I really have to go there? Even here, here in Nwemba, you feel his presence. Look at our up in the night, in the deep of it. Me I hear the white man humming there like Abua when his nose is filled with catarrh. How can you stop a man who hums in the sky from entering your village if he wants to? That is the way I see these things and when I see them like that I only laugh at Winjala when he says he can say no to the white man."

"Ever since you helped me once with your mpili drops, you think my nose has stayed that way," Abua said in joking protest. "But never mind. You talk like this about the white man when you have not even seen him in person. Wait until you see him…him and his woman, then you will know that Winjala does not want Nwemba to smile."

"This your man you talk so much about," Fosang challenged, "who does not even respect our up, is it when he comes here to Nwemba that he will see us like anything?"

"You do well to ask," Lobot with one eye supported.

Due regard meant a lot to Lobot. With his one eye gone, lost to the tip of a broomstick held by his little brother and into which he ran at full speed during a harmless playing session, he had grown to see a broomstick and its sharp destructive tip in everybody. The surviving eye had become alertly sensitive to other people's looks, words, gestures. It looked you up and down endlessly, opened and shut in quick succession as if to consume and digest the tangle of words and signs you produced. It was ever in search of the least sign of disdain, the slightest hint of anything less than full regard.

Whenever a remark was made that bore any link with a man's dignity, Lobot's ears pricked like those of an antelope that sensed a stalking tiger. He immediately thought of his one missing eye, how people turned away their faces and giggled or then laughed, or how others asked whether he had sold his eye to witchcraft. Fosang's question had that kind of effect on him. A man who hummed above the village at night without caring whether the village was asleep, without fearing to wake the gods, such a man, if he was ever allowed into the village, or if he forced his way into it the way he forced his way across the sky at night, would have only laughter and mockery for people like him.

"You do well to ask," he said again to Fosang.

"Winjala tells us that the white man does not look at people in Meamba like anything," Fosang added, "that the man he and Sama Gakoh worked for was a bit different, but that the other ones were bad people."

"You cannot depend on Winjala the Crude for who the white man is. Even his own brother Sama Gakoh with whom he worked in Meamba, did he look at him like anybody?"

"And what is bad about the white man?" Ntianop queried.

9

"And what is bad about the white man?" Fosang repeated, then asked: "Do you want to know? People who never open their houses to other people, who eat only when their doors are locked; people who count the pieces of meat before giving them to their cooks to prepare; women who throw their dirty things on men to wash…you call such people good people?"

"That is what Winjala has told you," Abua countered. "Why don't you say the things Sama Gakoh told you? You know I know them. Say them too."

"He cannot," Ntianop challenged. "If it comes to saying all the bad things about the white man he will talk from morning to night. Anyway, whether he tells Sama's side of the story or not, the next fishing contest will tell us when it reveals its decision."

"The coming contest. There they go again," Fosang said. "Who is afraid of the coming contest? Not Tankeh."

"And so you think it's Banda that is afraid?" Ntianop said, fighting back. "He has won once before and he will win this time again."

"Banda has won but Tankeh has never won," Lobot cut in sarcastically.

"Nobody has said Tankeh has never won," Abua corrected, "only that the second victory this time belongs to Banda."

"Because you want the white man's ways in Nwemba," Fosang quipped.

"Even the gods can see," Abua insisted, undeterred.

"No god will open his doors to his enemy," Lobot said with characteristic wisdom.

"No god will close his doors to his friend," Abua returned, delighted to draw even with him.

"All is in the second contest," Fosang cut in. "That's when we will know which way the gods lean."

Chapter Two

All these things I'm saying I'm saying in the white man's talk but in the way we talk in our own talk. When I talk our own talk in the white man's talk like this anyone who knows our talk will say this is not the white man's talk but the way they talk in Nwemba which they are now trying to put in the white man's talk.

Which is true. My head is a twin kolanut, one half the white man's talk, the other half our own talk in Nwemba.

Since I want to talk with you who are not people of Nwemba, I will use the white man half of my kolanut head. That white man half is very small. There are many, many things I will want to tell you but cannot because I do not know them in the white man's talk which is very small in my head. Those things are there in my head, many, wanting to be told. But how do I? They are there, sitting in the half of my head that only knows how we talk in Nwemba. If all of you understood the way we talk in Nwemba, I would say these things to you with all their roots. The white man's talk calls those roots details.

They are important, those details. If you cannot talk details in a talk, then you cannot catch a person's heart in that talk. And why talk to a person when his heart is standing somewhere and laughing at you and saying what is that one saying? He will just throw you and your talk without roots away. It is only through a man's talk that you can reach his heart, where he laughs, where he cries, where he smells the food, where he likes the girl, where he sees the sun, where he knows his brother.

11

Details.

The kerosene that gives light to the bush lamp. The roots that keep the tree in the ground. What is a tree without roots?

Roots.

Details.

Take our food.

Kehdjeu nann-nann

Kehdjeu nton-ton

Kehdjeu nkan-kann

Sam-kehdjeu

Senngwi

Nkann

Mbap-nduun

Makala

Nton

Nku

Mpa

Ghghann

Sanjap

Ngnn

Boh-lam

Tchuh

Tita-tchuh.

Mboh

Njanga-bann

Njanga-bonsuuh

Mlolo

Vuup

Kasinga

Nkoun-mali

Nkoun-fufuu

Wah

Njeh

Llann

Kuh-ntatitati

Kuh-ntonton

How can I talk to you about them? How can I bring water to your mouth? Even as I name them water comes to my mouth. My heart leaps. I smell the smell. The smell enters my nose. The pepper slaps my tongue. I wipe away the sweat.

Ngeng with bonsuh in ngwet-bann.

Sounds.

Yet that's where the heart is. A girl who puts ngeng with bonsuh in ngwet-bann before you does not open her mouth again. She has given you her heart. How can I tell you all this?

Will the white man too have his own ngeng with bonsuh in ngwet-ban? I'm asking this question like this, maybe he has even talked to me about it and wondered that my mouth remained dry and my heart did not jump.

He has. Otherwise how did Lucy talk to him? She must have placed something full of power before him and watched him quietly as he circled it with the eyes of a man after a heart…circled it, so that eating it became like taking the heart and putting it in his own heart for the two to become one.

If you see a man and a woman together, then their talk has a heart. Wherever. Whenever. You may not understand that talk, but it has a heart, roots.

The heart is in the talk.

And the talk is roots.

The white man half of my kolanut head is small. But I will use it. Or how do I talk with you who are not of my people? I may not be able to deliver the tree to you with its roots. Only bough and branches. Just take what I give you. That is all the white man half of my kolanut head can deliver. Maybe someday the way we talk in Nwemba will be the way we talk everywhere. When that day comes, I will talk to you the way we talk in Nwemba. That day I will deliver the tree to you with its roots.

The white man's head is not like my own. It is not divided into two halves like mine. It is only one and is full only of his own talk. The tree is complete with its branches and

13

roots. Not like my own tree that is without roots. So he can talk anywhere. And fully. And then we whose talk has no roots look at him like a magician, like somebody who knows how to talk. But it is only because no part of his talk has ever been taken away from him and replaced by something else that he does not understand.

This thing I am saying like this is very aching. I look at myself and it is just as if I had only one hand, not two; one leg, not two; one ear, not two; one eye, not two; one lip, not two; one row of teeth, not two. I feel that I am only half where the white man is full. He talks his language here; talks it there. When he enters your house he does not even ask you for your own language. He only starts talking his own. And then you forget yours. You do not even forget it. Once he enters your house, it is just as if you never had your own language.

It is not even as if because I have only half of the talk the white man has I can say half of the things he says in his talk. It is not like that. When you have only one leg instead of two, it does not mean that you can walk half as fast as somebody with two legs. You cannot walk at all. The man with two legs can jump over big holes; you with your one leg have to be carried for you to go from one place to the other, or then you hop along clumsily and only make people laugh at you. That is how I feel – like a man with one leg hopping and falling all the time and people laughing at me. And it is heavy. It is heavy for me to always think that the white man has all and I have nothing. Why must it be so? I have done everything to fight away that thought, that question, but it sits there quietly, even laughing at me. I have put all my power together and said no I will no longer think that I have nothing. I have clapped my eyes shut and pressed my lids until they pained, only because I want to say to myself that I too have something; that I too am somebody. But I have not succeeded.

14

Will I spend all my life struggling with another man's language at the same time as my own sits there idle, with no-one to talk it? This thought too pains me a lot. Is a language not a language only when it is spoken? Is there any other way you can make a language a language outside speaking it, outside using it to say the things that please you, the things that hurt you? Your little secrets, how can you share them if not in the tight corners of your own language where no man from outside can reach? Well, maybe I'm alone to feel this kind of pain, or maybe I'm not. But I cannot be alone. While in Meamba I saw many people who could not step aside and say something to each other that no other person could know. Just take Yaro and my father. If they had something to say to each other they used the white man's language...ah! the little they knew of it. How could you say many things in small language, I used to wonder. They always looked so helpless to me, just like the man with one leg.

My father was a washerman to the white man and his wife. He was not alone. Ikom Winjala also worked for them as yardman, and Lucas Yaro as cook and cleaner. Ikom and my father were from Nwemba, Yaro from Meamba.

Ikom Winjala's family and ours lived in two small houses opposite each other, separated from the white man's by a big orchard planted with fruit trees.

One would have thought, judging from the way the families fitted into the little houses, that the little houses were meant for our families — or was it our families that were meant for the little houses? They were both just a room and parlour each, not like the white man's own that looked so big from outside. I had never been inside, but from the way it looked outside, I kept thinking that the man and his wife could very easily get missing in it. How could such a big house be kept aside for just one man and his wife, no children? The man could be at this end and his wife at that

15

other end, he would have to shout and all the veins stand on his neck for the woman to hear.

Yaro the cook knew the inside of the house very well; every little corner of it. If he started talking about it, you could trek until water dries in your mouth and he would still not have finished.

Our own two little houses did not have anything much to be said about them, only a room and parlour. I do not know how Tankeh's father arranged sleeping in their own small house. In ours, our parents slept in the room and Lemea and I on mats at separate corners of the parlour, but not before we had moved things aside at bedtime to make room for our mats. I wonder how my parents would have managed us if our family had been bigger, say like Yaro's. Maybe that's one of the reasons why he lived in Ndongo quarter and not in the white man's compound where there was another small house next to our own, but empty. With two wives, the first with seven children and the second with five, how could he cram such a size into a room and parlour? He found enough accommodation for them in a five-bedroom house of iron sheets in Ndongo quarter not very far from his workplace. As cook to the white man, he could afford such a house. Not many other jobs paid so well. Just the fact even of cooking for the white man was enough to earn him any house of his wish in the town.

The size of his family was something that always fascinated me. I used to spend some afternoons there with Mo-Yaro. Mo-Yaro was his first son by his first wife. He was also my friend. What I admired about their household was the way you had to struggle to get your own share of food, from whichever branch. If you just sat there thinking that food would come and meet you, well. You had to go for the food; open pots and mortars, search the kitchen lockers; at times even peep under the parents' bed for choice portions. I found the game so exciting, most of all when

16

one child hid his ration and it was discovered and smoked off by another child. The loud cry and my food! ...let the person just put it back! And all of this dragging his ear at no-one in particular, and getting angrier the more no-one listened, or the more biting little snorts were thrown at him.

You did not need to leave the Yaros to find the different colours of life in another place. The family was complete in itself and provided all the charm, but also all the other side of charm, that you could find anywhere else. It was a family with colour and depth, and a father who sustained the home panache with occasional fits of drunkenness and all the pomp that such a mood could spill. Don't fear. This is still me talking the white man's talk. When I tie my banja I can talk the thing too. The only thing that pains me is that I am not tying my banja like this in my own talk. That is to say, eh, if it is in my own talk that I tie my banja like this, it will be come and hear.

In comparison, our own home looked too dry. Not really. Just that the excitement in Pa Yaro's home was not to be found in ours; at least not in equal measure. For one thing, my father hated the sight and smell of alcohol. That kind of man is always clear-headed; always careful and cautious, never surprised because never able either to surprise. And yet that's where most of the fun is: in surprises. He came home when he was expected home; sat where we knew he would sit, and went to bed almost at the same moment every evening. And once he was in bed we too had to lock up and sleep – or pretend to. Our own little house was drowned in calm.

I was forever at my father's neck for why our family was so small. I did not worry about Ikom Winjala's. I was only concerned about ours. Two children. Why only two of us? Was that the kind of number any father wanting to bear that name hoped for? Yaro for example had twelve children and was not stopping there by the looks of it. Mo-Yaro told me that they were gathering in more wood than usual because they were expecting a new small brother.

And us…what about us?

"Why is our own family so small, father?"

"Me, I don't care about numbers. You and your sister are enough for me. You see Ikom over there? He has buried over eight children. I don't want to spend my life by the graveyard. He wanted many children. He had them, and has buried all of them. Tankeh is the only one who has refused to go away."

"And mother, what does she say?"

"Is it your mother who makes the children? I make them."

"Or is it because of this small house?"

"We have not always lived here and we will not always live here. If I wanted more children I would take permission from the white man and move into Meamba, maybe to Ndongo quarter as Yaro has done. But that is not a big worry. My son, let me tell you. Before we came here from Nwemba I had it in mind to own a big family, eight, maybe nine children, with two or three wives if it became necessary."

"Not with mother alone?"

"If she could. But I was not going to marry the other women only for children. That's not why men marry many women. At least that's not the only reason. I was going to marry one or two other women to help your mother in other areas which you may not understand right now but which you will understand when you become a man."

"But you no longer think that way?"

"No, not ever since we moved here. Since I entered the white man's service I do not only work for him. I also watch the way he does his things."

"Even where children are concerned?"

"Yes, even concerning children."

"But he does not have even a single child."

"That's not true. He has two children, a boy and a girl.

18

He has talked to me about them and his wife has shown them to me on a piece of paper. They are in his country going to school, just as you were in Ediki-Mbeng. That is even why I accepted to let you go, so that you should follow in their footsteps. I looked at the white man's two children and said I too will remain with two, a boy and a girl, just like him. He never complained that his children were few. We should always watch what those people do. If they complain about something we should turn away from that thing. If they like something we should watch that thing closely. That's the way I have been watching how he does to his wife. Have you ever heard loud noises from their house as if he was shouting at his wife or beating her? When they are going out together he holds her hand. Their body is always touching. I find that very nice. If you like your thing, show it."

As I listened to him I thought of our own home and how he treated my mother. I remembered him saying once to her one evening when he had just finished his meal and was wiping the sweat from his face: "The best thing that can happen to a man is to have a woman he likes. You are my own that kind of woman." He had never raised his hand on her; and only very rarely spoke to her in a tone that betrayed anger. As I heard him talk about the white man and his wife it became clearer to me where he learnt how to treat his own wife.

"And Lemea, why did you not let her go with me to Ediki-Mbeng?"

"No, not my girl. The time has not come for me to remove my daughter from her mother's side. Maybe when you get married in the future your daughter will go to school. But that will be your time. Anything in its own time. I have nothing against people taking their daughters away from their mothers' side and sending them to the white man's school. But that is not my way. It is just like the white man's church up there on the hill. I may go there too one day, but for now it is not yet time."

19

"What do you know about that church? You have never set foot in it."

"I have not, but I know people who are there everyday. They say many things about the church, but what they say that I like is that the church says love your neighbour as yourself. I think that is good. If I ever have to go there it will be for this reason. Maybe when I go there two times and I like it, I will take Winjala there the third time. He needs to hear that kind of message."

In our little house talk like this gave our small family the sense of bigness that our actual numbers starved us of, so that with time I did not mind at all if other children laughed at me for having only one sister whom nobody ever saw, and no brother to rely on where there was a fight. Unfortunately for most of them who laughed at me, I put dust in their mouths easily whenever they challenged me to a fight. That was not what I needed other brothers for. I wanted to be able to hold hands with them on our way back from school, help carry their bags as I saw other children doing, share funny stories and secrets, do so many other things that one could only do with one's brothers and sisters. The loneliness beat me more than any fight.

I felt sorry for Tankeh's father and even for Tankeh himself. To have lost so many children, so many brothers and sisters, was surely a sad memory to live with. I now understood why he kept to himself so much. He went to the wrestling ground only to sharpen his skill, not really for the company that wrestling gave him. Immediately after each fight he ran back to their own little house and nobody saw him again until he stepped out to bird-hunt in the orchard. And even then he did not talk to you if you saw him.

Not that anyone was dying to talk to him. The air between our two families was not good – that was the least one could say. My father thought Ikom had his eyes too much on the white man's things; Ikom for his part treated my father with scorn. Many times he had stood before our little house and howled insults at our entire house, calling my father the white man's thing, a dung-eater and saying many other foul things. With a man like that you could not keep a good relationship. My father rarely ever answered back, which I found both surprising and even irritating. Dung-eater. I knew dung to be the droppings of animals, not of men. How my father could maintain his calm in the face of such insult amazed me. But he did, and even explained.

"There he goes again," he once said to us as we were gathered inside and the thing was pouring from Ikom's mouth in front of our house. "He wants me to talk but I will not. In this life you see like this, no matter how angry a person is, listen to him, patiently. He will soon grow angry at his own anger and leave you alone. But if you meet his anger with anger, you feed his anger and he gets angrier. And you too. I will not answer Ikom. I do not like his ways and I have said so to him. That's the only answer I can give him. He can call me all kinds of names, it will not change what I think of him."

We the children carried on this standoff at our own level. I had fought thrice with Tankeh, and pulled Lemea's hair at least once for clapping when he threw Njitifuh in a fight. What kind of girl was this? The same boy whose father calls yours a dung-eater. That's the boy you clap for. I had pulled her hair hard and she had fled screaming into the house and saying when a boy fights well I have the right to clap for him, or something like that, which had sent me chasing after her again and only stopping in front of a bolted door from behind which some more offensive things were being said.

Ikom could stay in his house for three, four days and not bother to take out his machete and clear the white man's orchard or where his animals lived. With that kind of attitude I could understand why he called my father the white man's thing, among other foul names. My father left our little house each day to the white man's big house where he spent the day washing his things.

Not many will understand what this means – a washerman to a white man.

Washerman?

Yet that's how close you get to being a white man yourself. If you touch the same clothes a white man wears, then you become somehow a white man yourself. If you do the things a white man does, then you become a white man yourself. The way I think about this thing, being a white man is not looking like him but doing like him. If you ask me that is the way I think.

My father touched the white man's clothes, removed the dirt from them. It was like he washed the white man, made him clean. If we only look at the clothes, we can say my father was even whiter than the white man: what the one made dirty the other made clean again. That's the way I understand these things. If you make a dirty thing clean then you are bigger in the eyes of that thing than the one who only puts dirt on it. Ask that thing who it will run to in trouble and you will see.

My father did not only wash the white man's clothes. He washed his wife's own too, even the ones she wore closest to her body.

He had never seen the things a woman wore closest to her skin. Not to mention touching them.

He told us how he found it difficult at the beginning, but how he became used to it later, to the point that he started whistling when washing the woman's inner things. He washed them everyday because she put them in the washing basket everyday.

But the first day was not easy for him. He said it in a big laugh lined with pain.

"O ho! ho! Sama, son of Gakoh. Ask your mother whether I know what she wears near her skin... I mean just know it. So what was I to do with that kind of thing from another woman's body? I left the basket standing there till the sun was about to go down, only washing the man's things which I washed slowly so that they could last the whole day. From time to time I stretched my back and looked at the basket."

The tale was painful but my father covered the pain with the kind of laugh that a man laughs when something strong hits him.

"Even when I finished the man's things I did not immediately drag the basket with the woman's things to my front. I sat down for a long period hoping to give myself some rest, but the basket kept looking at me. I waited until the sun closed its eyes, then I took the basket and dumped everything in it into a basin of water without sorting them out by colour as I did with the man's clothes."

My mother kept this day in her head. Without knowing what exactly had happened to my father her husband on that day of work in the white man's house, she sensed all the same that it had not been a day like other days. First he turned aside her greetings of welcome, then he threw himself on his bed and propped his head on his two palms and looked at the ceiling for long periods.

"I came and sat by him," my mother recalled. "And I asked him many times and quietly what had happened but he would not say."

"Say?" my father now asked. "What did you want me to say? That I had spent the day cleaning the things a woman wears near her skin? How could I even start saying a thing like that?"

Only Lemea did not see anything wrong with the kind of work her father did. Maybe her little age shielded her from the sensitive corners of a man's life, or that she just was not observant enough to see the rejection that accompanied every word my father spoke on this particular experience. The kind of questions she asked him showed that the things in her head were not the things of childhood innocence.

"Papa, and the things the man wore close to his body?"

"No, I always washed those ones."

"Did they feel different when you washed them?"

"What kind of question is that you are asking your father?"

Even this rebuke from her mother did not seem to have any effect on her.

"Mama, don't stop me."

"You can't be asking your father that kind of question."

"Are we not conversing?"

"Even in conversation you mind the kind of things you say, especially the kind of questions you ask."

At this Lemea kept quiet, but one could see that she was sulking more than she was obeying her mother.

Later it became different. He also sorted the woman's things out and grouped them by colour, or by how dirty they were.

Her field trousers were often quite dirty, especially at the knees, since she knelt a lot. But he said the things she wore close to her skin were often very clean. Only once did he have to steep one of them in boiled water to remove bloodstains. Otherwise washing the woman's inner things was light work. She was a good woman, so he thought maybe she just wanted him to earn money without doing too much heavy work.

Washing the woman's things was just one finger out of the ten that were my father's working life. There were many other things he did for the white man and which brought him satisfaction and us joy. For one thing, the man and his wife had no problem with my father's character as a person.

Nothing surprising. He was a man anybody would like. And his best admirer was his wife who never forgot the quiet way he swept her off her feet. Never forgot. And this many years after their marriage.

"This my man…" she recalled fondly, "he never talked to me. But each time I heard him talk to others I was dying. It was with him that I knew a voice could kill a woman. And I was not alone. Many girls in Nwemba said they could just die because of his voice. Then one day I saw Pa Gakoh in my father's house. This your father you see like this."

"Chei! Mama!" Lemea pouted in her direction.

"My daughter, it is good that your head and your feet and your heart be in one place. I looked at the boys in the village and the only one I saw was your father. Not riches or strength. Just a good, warm voice. A man with a good, warm voice cannot be a bad man. Riches don't talk; and strength can be brutal at times. But a warm voice has only itself to offer."

"Mama, you looked for the right thing," her daughter said.

"Eh, my daughter. Was I wrong? Does that voice not cover us all like a blanket, even today?"

"And what if Pa Gakoh did not come to your father?"

"I would have gone where my father sent me, but with a heavy heart."

"Don't tell me he was the only one who came."

"Not that. Many of them came, but it was Pa Gakoh's cup that I accepted in my hands."

"I never knew him."

"Not even your brother knew him. He died shortly after I entered your father's house. I was only a few months with your brother in me. But you see your father? As he is, that's how your grandfather was."

"Mama, let me ask you a question. In your days, when you liked a boy how did you let him know?"

25

"You kept it to yourself."

"And died with it?"

"And died with it. But not always. At times the parents of the boy you liked came to see your parents. Then you accepted their cup in your hands. But it did not always happen like that. Many times you sat in your mother's house and listened to the voices in your father's house and they were not the voices you were hoping for."

"And what did you do at such times?"

"You put your face in your hands and cried, and your mother who was always watching shouted at you and said how you had no say in the decision that came from your father's house."

"So you were lucky."

"I was lucky. But why do you ask me these questions?"

"Maybe I should not have asked them."

"Why? But only that things have not changed very much."

"But I want to be as lucky as you."

"The man you like may not be the one who sends his father to see your father."

"I will not wait for him to send his father to papa."

"Eh?"

"I will not wait."

"Eh, my daughter?"

"Mama, I will talk to him."

"To him?"

"The boy."

"Thank the spirits for your little age."

"Mama, even though I don't leave this house I see things."

Lemea was such an enigma. No-one ever knew where her own way of talking came from. Even the other little girls she played with always said she talked like a woman whose head was full of quacha. Only such a head would face the boys at the playgrounds, as Njitifuh learnt one sunny afternoon.

This young man was in the habit of leaving the boys' playgroup and coming to tease the girls or wipe their tabala design on the ground. Each time the girls saw him coming they dispersed and hid in their houses for those who could reach them, or in the nearest plantain bush, until he did what he wanted with their playthings and designs on the ground and returned gleefully to his group.

Lemea too would run away each time she saw or heard him whistling provocatively towards them. She ran like that a couple of times. Then one day, without saying anything to any of the other girls she refused to run again.

Even Njitifuh was not expecting this. His biggest fun was not in wiping off the tabala designs on the ground with his feet but in seeing how the girls scampered off, some of them falling and wounding their knees or their arms and rising in confusion and running crying into their houses. His greatest pleasure was to see some of the frightened girls actually miss their own houses and run into a different house. He would laugh and hold his sides and laugh again, and the rest of the boys would laugh along with him.

But Lemea had decided not to run again. This day Njitifuh started coming as usual with his lips gathered offensively, whistling a kind of whistle that had no sense in it but that was meant only to say I am coming. He came just when the girls were caught in the excitement of the last throw, the one that decided the winner and sent them all shouting with joy and jumping round the pitch and allowing their little skirts to fly in the wind and expose their empty bottoms.

First the little girls sighed, their excitement plucked suddenly from them, then they set off towards their different houses. Lemea stepped into the tabala box and stood there, deaf to the frightened shouts of Leme don't stand! Leme run! Run!

First the whistling dried on Njitifuh's lips, then his steps slowed. But he continued forward, groping almost, as if with jaundiced eyes.

The little girls came out of their hiding again and ventured closer to their playground, but far enough to run back into safety if it came to that. The boys stepped backwards instead, as if pushed by some wind that had not always been there.

Njitifuh's steps had slowed so that he was now only picking them. The distance between him and Lemea was becoming narrower and narrower. He stopped and tried to frighten her into a run with wild noises and gestures, but she did not even see his gimmicks. The boys moved further away from their playground, and the girls closer back to theirs. This time they did not stand in isolated corners. They closed in together and stood touching one another with new defiant faces.

Njitifuh turned and looked at where his playmates had been standing and found that they had all receded to a distance twice as long as the one from their playground to the playground of the girls; that they had moved back so far that he could not even see their eyes again, only their heads which did not seem to be facing in any known direction. He turned as if he had forgotten something and paced back towards the boys' playground with shouts of jubilant relief following him, and looks of wonder waiting for him where his playmates had moved back to.

Tankeh was among the boys for once.

Njitifuh's return chocked the boys' heads with revenge. All of them screamed for a punitive raid on the girls. Only Tankeh said no, that he had watched the happening carefully and failed to see where the girl went wrong.

With a girl who could do things like that, I was not surprised that she asked her father the kind of questions she asked. He was talking about washing the things a woman wore closest to her body and all she could ask was whether the things the man wore closest to his own body felt different from those the woman wore.

If you had a girl like Lemea as a sister, you never slept with your both eyes shut fast, or get up and see that she had blown the roof over your head. There was a little factory in Ediki-Mbeng that turned out rubber shoes non-stop. Lemea's head was like that factory. It turned out ideas non-stop, one idea as strange as the other, so that looking at her was like looking down the muzzle of a gun.

Chapter Three

The white man was called Harrington. Pete Harrington. And his wife's name was Lucy. He used to go out everyday carrying strange things he called field instruments. I don't know me how to describe them. You can only describe the things you know or which look like something you know. These things the white man carried everyday did not look like anything I had ever seen. So I cannot describe them. But I can call some names: kamra, lensiz, bainokiulaz. These ones did not talk. He had two things that talked. One was a seliula foun, another a lep tap.

The seliula foun was a small thing which he held in his hand close to his ear. He was a big man with the hands of a tapper and when he held that foun near his ear and was talking to it and it was talking to him too, if you only looked at the two of them from far, you knew that he was talking to his big hand and the big hand was talking to him too. You had to come closer and look at his big hand well and then you would see the little foun buried in it and talking to him.

As for the second one, he carried it on his thighs like a hungry child crying, and opened its big looking glass and looked at it at the same time as his fingers danced on the lower part as if on a luung. At times too that one sang; but on the whole it was silent and only the man looked at the looking glass from time to time like at his face and then murmured as his head went from one end of the looking glass to the other.

To me this man was a medicine man.

He drew a lot. Mainly birds. But also butterflies. He seemed to be after everything that flew on wings.

His wife too went out a lot. But unlike the man who searched the sky, she liked to look into the earth. It was as though they had divided the property of the spirits among themselves, he with the sky, she with the earth. She liked to dig up little things from the earth and hold them in her white hands and look at them closely. She would come back in the evening with a bag full of things without name, which she spread on a large table and threw into little groups and pinned papers in the middle of each group.

The white man did not like Ikom Winjala very much. He said there was something about the man that made liking him very difficult. What it was he did not say. "I can only just about tolerate him," he usually said. One thing he also said which I found difficult to understand was that in addition to not liking Winjala, he respected him. I found this hard to understand. How could you not like a man and at the same time respect him? He said he had observed Winjala closely and found that he had something in him that no-one could change, and that thing was his sense of who he was. He said most people in his own country were like that. They knew that the world had to come to them and not them to go to the world, and that if the world came to them it left what it brought with it outside and took only what they said and did. He had that kind of feeling about Ikom Winjala, feelings of a man who knew where he put his foot, who left a troubling impression of being on top, in command, even from down where he stood.

The white man's work with birds he shared with liking other animals. To show how he liked these other animals, he built a fence in one corner of his big compound and put some in it: one green snake, a tortoise, a deer and a baby monkey, each one with its own place where it lived. Birds too also came in many numbers to eat some of the food given to the animals. This made the white man very happy. At times he jumped among the birds like a drunk dancer to mbaghalem.

The birds knew his smell well. When he jumped among them they did not fly away. They only continued to jump from here to there and pick up small bits of food in their mouths. Some even allowed him to carry them and put them against his jaw and speak to them.

Once I too threw some food in front of our little house for the birds to visit me and I take them in my hands and talk to them. They did not. They only went to the fence built by the white man.

He used to tell us about how he spent long hours in a place called Trfag Skwe in his country feeding little pieces of their own kind of food to their own kind of birds, some of which he said looked very much like our own birds. He called some of them pijns and others davs, and said he had seen many of their type in Ediki-Mbeng and also a few in Meamba and on the land between the two places.

Later when I went to the big school in Ediki-Mbeng and saw the way these two birds were written, the first bird especially, I wondered why the white man's talk could write one thing and say another thing. Pigeon. Pijn. Why not just write it the way they said it? Maybe these people I was seeing like this could be people who at times said one thing and did the other thing. There was a name in our own talk for such people: ghan wubli. You never knew what lay in their belly. A thing that left their belly on its way out changed its form before it came out. If it was darkness, it changed into day before it came out, so that even if you heard day, what they had in their belly was night. You fell into their trap of friendship very easily, and only put your two hands on your head later.

Harrington liked the baby monkey in a special way. It was always the last animal he talked to before leaving his house, and the first he went to on return.

A strong friendship tied them together. The baby monkey started dancing long, long before we saw the white man himself, so that my father no longer looked down the road to know whether the white man was coming, but at the baby monkey who was now even more important to him than the master he worked for.

The yardman had strict instructions never to enter the animals' area. His duty was only to cut the grass near the living place of the white man's friends and burn it far, but never to enter where they lived.

But the washerman could enter their living place at any time. In addition to washing the clothes of the white man and his wife, he also took food and water to the animals and cleaned their living place.

The baby grew quickly into a big animal. The white man was so happy with this that he soon started to cut down his field trips so that he could spend more time with his big friend. He told us that studying our birds also made him discover what real happiness was.

He named his baby friend Stirrup.

One day my father gathered courage and asked him the meaning of that name and he said something about climbing a horse; but that he gave the name because he liked the way it sounded; that it reminded him of getting out of sleep, things like that.

Harrington returned from a trip to Ediki-Mbeng one day and found Stirrup's house empty. He called my father angrily and questioned him. My father said Sa, Winjala…a see he witi mukuta wey blot di komot fo dey and that from that day Winjala had not returned to work again, at which Harrington exclaimed many times: "Crude! Crude Winjala!"

All this happened with me in Ediki-Mbeng where the white man had sent me to secondary school. Shortly after my return he retired my father and we returned to our village.

Before we returned to Nwemba the white man told my father that he would have loved to keep me longer in secondary school in Ediki-Mbeng and why not send me to his country for more studies, but he had decided against all that in favour of my returning to our village where he was sure I would be of greater use; also that if I encountered any difficulties there I should write to him.

He did not say anything about my sister. I'm not even sure he knew anything about the existence of the little girl with a head like the rubber shoe factory in Ediki-Mbeng. The way his compound was laid out, it was possible for him to live all his life in it and never know his workers' families. The main house in which he lived looked outwards towards the centre of Meamba while the little houses in which we lived were dotted in the back, at a good distance, and shaded from immediate view by a bushy orchard.

My father kept Lemea away from the knowledge of the white man. She stayed in the house with our mother and spent the day between our small house and the small kitchen shed behind. At least that was what she was supposed to do; and that was the way her father thought she spent her days. But a girl with a head like her own could not reduce her days to simply watching her mother cook and to other things like fetching the dishes and adding wood under the cooking pot.

Each time I came back from school, especially in the first days, she picked up my bag and opened the books with pictures and looked at them with shining eyes. There was one book she liked very much. That one had the drawing of children in a classroom and a little girl showing up her hand to the class mistress. She was the only child in the class with her hand up, and her face was lighted by a big smile that showed all her new teeth. Lemea always looked at this picture for long. If it was a calabash of palmwine and she a man, she would drink it and drink it and never get

35

drunk. She remained everyday with her mother in the small kitchen, but her head was in many other places, with that little girl in the book, with the other girls in the playground; and with the boys too.

Talking about the boys, Tankeh was a stay-at-home type too who spent all his time roaming the white man's orchard and shooting his birds, with his father's encouragement. He knew all the different birds that flew in and out of the orchard, what fruits each kind ate, and the best moments to let go the charge from his catapult. The hunting was not only for sport; it was equally for necessity since it provided the home with much-needed meat. Ikom was known to smile between two mouthfuls and laugh at the white man for his bizarre relationship with the birds.

"The man leaves his country to come here and look at birds as if they were his brothers and sisters." Then he would add, talking to his son: "Sharpen your hunting. You will become a man through it. When we return to Nwemba it is hunting that will put food before you. Today the birds; tomorrow the deer. That's how you grow up. What you teach yourself can never be taken away from you. What the gods give you will remain yours forever. Like this grass I cut. No matter what the white man does, he can never own it. He came and met it; he will go and leave it. Sharpen your skills and hunt the birds. Let nobody ever fool you that the birds belong to the white man. He did not bring any birds into Meamba. He came and met them here. He will go and leave them to us."

When Tankeh was not hunting in the orchard he was wrestling with other boys on an open piece of ground behind the plumtree that marked the limit between the white man's compound and Ndongo quarter.

From the little kitchen behind our house one could see the open space sufficiently clearly to distinguish the boys locked in combat. Lemea was in the habit of taking the dirty things behind the kitchen for washing. Each time I was returning from school that's where she was, with the dirty things piled before her and little or no washing going on, especially when the wrestling was in full session. No matter how hard mother talked to her about that practice of taking things behind the kitchen, she would not change. The whole thing got even worse if Tankeh Winjala was one of the wrestlers. She would abandon the dirty things where she dumped them and move closer to the wrestling ground, but not close enough to be seen by any of the boys. If Tankeh won, which was almost always, she would then hurry back and settle to her washing. If he lost, the dishes remained in all their dirt so that mother had to go behind the kitchen herself and wash the ones she needed and hope that when I returned from school I would finish the rest. Once Lemea had made up her mind that she was not washing any dishes, nothing would make her go back to those dishes.

Many times I was tempted to tell the white man that I had a sister who shared the excitement of my books with me. Once I even told him the story of a little girl who dreamed of school so much that she escaped from home to find work in a headmaster's house where she could be near schoolchildren and drink some of their knowledge. He listened with interest but did not ask to know who that little girl was, much to my disappointment. I wanted to tell him that the little girl could jump out of my story and become a real little girl that he could take by the hand to the school she dreamed of. But he didn't ask.

Chapter Four

Winjala the Crude returned to Nwemba and found his house on the ground with ants living in the bamboos.

The day he arrived he sat in the ruins and looked at the other houses as they stood proudly in the sun. Anger and sadness filled him, and he bowed his head and mumbled: "I am back in my village, but I am homeless." He bit his lips, then added: "My house fell because I left it and went to work for the white man. I made a mistake."

My uncle Abua saw what had happened and offered him a house in his compound where he could live until his fallen house was up again. The day he came to Winjala with the offer the newcomer sat him under a plum tree not far from the ruins and said to him: "You are giving me a house today because you built it and stayed here to look after it."

"You built too. Only that yours has fallen."

"Where was I when it was falling?"

"Why? You were working for the white man."

"And what have I brought back?"

"That work fed your family."

"Who is happier today, I who went to work for the white man or you who stayed here in your village and took care of your house?"

"Winjala, those two things each have their own place. You who went to work for the white man achieved something. Those of us who stayed behind in our village achieved our own thing."

39

"What have I brought back from serving the white man? What? Even the house I left behind is no longer standing?"

"You cannot think of what you gained only in terms of this house that has fallen. Think also of the many other things which you learnt from the white man and which those of us who stayed here do not know. Remember my own days there."

Winjala let go a tiny smile, then said reminiscing: "When you traded in dry fish."

"Yes, you remember those days, so when I talk about the white man it is the talk of someone talking about pear with the thing in his mouth."

Winjala never wanted to hear that. His whole body seemed impervious to anything that put the white man in a positive light.

"Abua, what has the white man put in your heads?"

"Nothing that he has not put in your own head."

"The white man cannot put anything in my head."

"At least you worked for him and received his orders."

"I cut grass. That grass is not different from the grass in my farm. It is not his grass. He did not bring any grass here."

"He brought other things which you use."

"That is what you will always say. He also met things here which he uses."

"His medicine house."

"Did we not have medicine places? Do we not still? And our birds. What does he want behind them?"

"He is learning things about them that you and I will never know."

"Thieves. Those people are all thieves. Each time he touches any of our birds he turns them into nothing birds."

"Your birds run away from you."

"Ha! ha! That's how they can remain real birds, not the woman birds we have now because a white medicine man has spoiled their heads."

"Show out your hand too let me see whether any bird will stand on it."

"Why do you want me to change our birds into woman birds, nothing birds? That is what the white man does to anything he touches. He changes it into a woman thing. Look at all the people in Meamba. They are like women now. Since the other one in a long white kaba came and started talking to them in the ngomba house he built, they have all become women. Is that what you want the people of Nwemba to be?"

This last way of talking won many people to Winjala's side. The men shook with fear when they thought of what would happen to them if the white man came into the village; how he would come from nowhere and transform all of them into women; and before doing that he would first gather their animals into one corner of the village and stop the villagers from going near them or hunting even those still in the forest – that was a thought which not many of them allowed to remain for long in their heads.

"And where would the spirits of the land be?" the deeply perplexed ones asked. "Would they just remain quiet and see their own children go in no time from men who wielded spears into women who sat frightened at one corner of the house and only did what the white man said?"

Chief Ndelu heard the argument raging between Abua and Winjala without saying anything. When asked why he was not saying anything, he replied that Abua and Winjala were both his subjects. Ikom Winjala, you are right, or Abua Gakoh, you are right. That was not him. He could not come between his subjects and throw one out and keep the other. He said Chief Lahmi of Meamba, great grandson of Walang the affable, had boasted to him more than once about the good things the white man had brought to his village, but that he did not borrow other people's feet in his own race.

His two subjects had come to him, each with his own position. Both of them had talked with force, one perhaps a bit more than the other, so that if he only based his decision on the way they talked, he would say the white man should never come to Nwemba. But it was not so easy. He was a man of good judgment despite his young age, and knew that quite often there were more good things in what was not said than in what was said. It was his thinking, also, that any decision taken without the guiding hand of time also fell down quickly. So he refused to support any of his two subjects against the other.

It was in this climate that we returned to Nwemba.

Our first days were difficult. I was sad to hear how the villagers talked about my father. They said he was worse than a woman; that a man who touched the things a woman wore closest to her body was worse than the woman who wore them.

My father found these things painful. But they did not surprise him. He could not blame the villagers for thinking that way. In our village a man did not go near the things a woman wore closest to her body, or to anything she wore even. So he did not blame the villagers.

Instead, he blamed the man who told them those things without explaining that out of Nwemba men could do certain things and still remain men. He washed the things the white woman wore closest to her body. But that did not make him a woman. He washed those things with his hands, not with his body. Those things did not touch him as a man. Washing them was not different from cutting grass as Winjala the Crude did, or cooking food as Lucas Yaro did. He washed the white woman's things to earn money. In Meamba you had to do something to earn money, or else you collected your wife and children and returned to your village, as he had just done. From the time the white man said he no longer wanted to keep him, he knew that time to return to the village had come. You did not stay in a place like Meamba if you did not work and earn money. Washing the things the white woman wore was work. The man talking to the villagers had to say these things to them too. That was the way he thought.

Once Ntianop came visiting and my father bared his mind to him.

"The things I hear since I returned trouble me a lot. Why should Winjala tell the village only one thing out of many things that he knows? I also washed the white man's things. Why does he not say that? Why does he only press on the woman's things I washed? And what is wrong in washing a woman's things if that can feed my family? Look at my hands. Have I lost a finger because I washed the things worn by a woman? I washed things worn by a good woman. This to me is important. There were other white women in Meamba. I know at least two other ones whose washermen I met in the meeting of workers for white men. Their own washermen did not say good things about them. One used to say how his own white woman inspected the things he washed and then threw them in his face shouting that they were not clean and that he was stupid and could not tell a clean thing from a dirty one. The other man's white woman did not do that but she gave him things to wash that at times took away his appetite for many days. Madam Lucy was a different kind of white woman. She spoke to me softly and never criticized what I did. And because of this I washed her things as if they were my own things I was washing. I used to hold them up against the sun and inspect them for any dirt stains that hid from me."

He said how at times she would come to the laundry place and stand at a distance and watch him as he washed the things. She said she liked to see the white foam on his dark hands. She never said black hands. She always said dark hands. That she liked the way the foam stood on his dark hands as he squeezed the clothes.

He remembered how once she appeared suddenly in the laundry place when he thought she was on her field trip. "She came just when I had emptied her own things into the big basin and was pressing them into the water. This time she did not stand far away. She came close to me and stood watching. I could smell the smell of the air coming out of her mouth. This was the first time I smelt the air from a white woman's mouth. I swallowed it the way the drinkers swallow warm kwatcha, and for a while the washing turned into a dance. She bent and held one of my hands, this one, as it came out of the water with foam on it. 'I want to know how you do it. You squeeze the clothes with so much power, yet they don't tear,' I heard her say close to my ears."

He remembered how he put her two hands on her own underwear and showed her the way to wash it clean… how she laughed repeatedly as his hands and hers went in and out of the basin.

"And he," he said softly at the end of his account, talking about Winjala, "he has filled the village with wrong stories. He left Meamba in shame but has not said so. Instead he carries my name all over and drags it in mud. Nwemba knows that I am the last of women, and he the biggest bringer of meat!"

"You know his sweet tongue," Ntianop said in sympathy. "Don't blame us for believing him. He brought more meat on his back than Nwemba had seen for long. To us he had to be a hunter of a different kind. He boasted to us: 'You don't kill a monkey like the one I brought back to Nwemba just jumping about in front of your house. You go far, far into the forest and spend many days there, bringing down the heaviest monkey with one throw of your spear. You bury your spear in the ribs of the biggest monkey; bury it so deep it does not move a foot again. Then you fight off the rage of the survivors and carry home your kill. The forest lies far, far from Meamba, in the direction of Ediki-Mbeng.

44

Many days to go, many other days to return.' Then he changed his voice and continued: 'Those who spend their days with their hands buried in the dirty water from things worn by women are just women themselves. There is work for men in Meamba. And when you do the right kind of work you return to your own village with your head high. And you walk around the village proudly. You can cut grass for the white man. It is not his grass. It is the grass in your farm; it is the same grass in your village; it is the grass in which you hunt. When you cut grass you remain a man. When you hunt you remain a man. You do not go to Meamba to be changed by the white man into a woman. You do not go there to run when his woman coughs and to spend days in the sun washing the dirt from the things she wears closest to her skin."'

My father heard all these things and refused to answer. Only the coming to Nwemba of the things he had seen in Meamba, the things of the white man, would answer for him. Ikom Winjala was a strong talker, especially cup in hand. My father could not match him in that. But things were not always only about talking; or only about drinking. My father did not drink; not ever since as a young man he drank palmwine once and spent the rest of the night looking for the way to his house. He always laughed each time he heard men say the truth was in the cup. He was more interested in the way, and used to combine both views into one and use it on himself: "The truth is I lost my way in the cup." And to him you could not hold the cup and still find your way.

But there were times I wished he held the cup, however occasionally. I can say this today because I am grown up. I have drunk palmwine and its effect has pushed me to a level of understanding and perception quite simply out of my reach in other moments. Under the influence of palmwine my eyes have gained the sharpness of four eyes, my head the intelligence of two heads. I have stood up to situations that would otherwise have drowned me if I had faced them without the supporting influence of palmwine. That my father did not drink deprived him of a few advantages in his perception of life. Because his blood was always calm, he saw life as a straight line with no dents and curves, made up only of truths and moments of gladness. And when the curves appeared suddenly ahead of him, he went straight into the bush.

I don't know who ever told him that you lived with other people as if they were your carbon copies who thought and acted just like you. That was not how things were. He had lived with people like Ikom long enough to know this. Maybe if he had been accustomed to some palmwine, he would have stood in front of his little house in Meamba and thrown Ikom's dung back in his face. He instead gathered us together in the house and talked about not being angry when everyone else around you was angry; that they would grow tired of being angry and leave you alone. That talk entered my ear this way and went out the other way. There were times in this life you see like this that you needed some palmwine.

My father carried his own truths to the chief, whom he knew to be a leader with a good ear. No waste of time trying to counter Winjala. He wouldn't be able to.

But even though he sought the Chief's judgment, the things the village said ate him inside bit by bit. They were like spear-ends striking repeatedly on the same spot. A hole opened in his heart which every villager's talk made deeper. He would not have minded if they took what he said before throwing him away as they were doing. He would not have felt it so much. They could have said to him: "We want the ways you are talking to us about, but we will not allow them to turn us into women as they have turned you." Talk like that he would have taken happily. But nobody sent his head that way.

Wherever he went the only talk was that he was a woman. If two men stood, he could not stand with them and share their talk. They would look away and laugh without saying why they were laughing.

To visit his brother Abua he had to wait until night came.

Even the women too started to talk like the men. In their meetings they asked my mother questions that tied a bundle in her neck. Some wanted to know whether my father continued to wash the white woman's things even when she was seeing her moon. These questions they asked in laughter that hurt.

My mother said to them that her man was still a man, but would they listen? Their own men had spoiled their heads. Some of them even blamed my father for the new ways of their own men:

"My man shows me now that he can drink."

"With mine, it is now his hand that talks in place of his mouth."

"Sama Gakoh. Who brought him back?"

Soon my father lay in his bed and did not get up again. In the first days he could talk. Then one day he called me to his side, early in the morning, and held my hand and said with difficulty: "The contest...my daughter..." Tears were falling from his eyes. As the tears fell he held my hand faster. His lips moved but he could not talk. He was facing Meamba.

Chapter Five

Chief Ndelu found no reason to hurry a decision, now that the two men had died. Why not put the matter to the custodians of the land, those same ones who provided life? If he only followed the opinions he heard among his subjects he would go in one direction that may not be the one he wanted to follow.

Why even trouble himself when the fishing contest was there? Wasn't it during that contest that the river spirits sat in council over the destiny of the village and showed him and his people which way to go? He would throw the matter to the gods and submit himself to their decision. They knew best. If they wanted the white man to come to the village, they would tell him; if they did not want the white man to enter Nwemba, they would say so. The gods of Nwemba did not have one eye only. They did not have only two. Each of their sons was an eye. The gods saw what the sons saw.

And they saw best in the fishing contest, when they put their eyes together and through the winner told the Chief, their own eye above the ground, what they saw. So the things he heard among his subjects did not bother him much. My father's death saddened him, but he was confident that the gods who saw everything were going to say if he died for nothing or for something.

Perhaps he would not depend only on the gods in this matter. Which way the village went was in the hands of the gods, but now he was ready to say it was not in their hands only. He had depended solely on them in the past and had seen that the message they sent him through the winner did not bring only good things. And his people had suffered.

The year of Fofang's victory did not bring good fortune to Nwemba. The draught came and the animals fled to shades in far-away forests. He remembered this, and how his people's suffering put pain in his heart. To bring back the rains he did a thing he had never done before. He dug out the remains of the victory goats and repeated the ritual all over. He begged the gods and begged them again. Still the rains did not come. Then one day, when he was not expecting it, the rains came, and the animals returned from their exile. He never forgot that year. He would put the matter to the gods at the next fishing contest, but he would also be ready to depend on what his own head told him.

Since the Chief's decision to seek the sanction of the gods, I had become a permanent concern to Tankeh Winjala, son of Winjala the Crude. He saw in me a rival, and suspected everything I did. He liked to drag me into battle, as if to win before the time. That was how we came to fight the last fight. I never provoked a fight, but I never ran away from one.

As you turn into Nwemba from Tazim, you reach a fork in the road five bamboo sticks away that divides your steps into two sides, one taking you to Chief Ndelu's compound and the other to the heart of the village. The place is covered in shrubs, in dry as in rainy season – a most unusual kind of place in a village that wears its brown skin like the hoarse sack of a masquerade dancer. It is at this point that we fought, against the setting dry season sun.

The red sun, swept over partly by a lazy cloud, peeped and dogged, ready to lift the winner before continuing to bed. When a winner finally came, people were excited, not a few of them happy. It showed on their faces, in the way they balanced the smiles on them, like bubbles they were afraid to lose.

Some of the people liked the ground duel, others the mid-air tussle. But it was the deciding throw that attracted the most attention. Maybe if it had gone a different way, not many people would have liked it or talked that much about it so many days afterwards; but the way it went, there seemed to be something in it that brought good feelings to many hearts, warm words to most lips.

As people voiced their impressions about what they had just seen, they drifted away, dry leaves in the breeze. They did not break up, each on his own, but went in bunches, in little clusters, some the size of a family, others that of a wrestling team.

Only Olembe hurried home, but not before he'd shouted to everyone's hearing that the evening's harvest would be abundant and sweet.

Each group had its own tale of the fight to tell.

One group, the one at the head of which Sendelenghi placed himself, held up a lively account of what they had just witnessed. Sendelenghi talked most and his own account seemed to point to another event, not the one they were just from seeing. So there was a lively exchange.

"Tankeh gave Banda dust to eat," Sendelenghi celebrated.

"And Banda filled Tankeh's mouth with grass," Masutu retorted.

"Like a goat," another one concurred. The rest of the group, about seven in number, broke into laughter. Some said I treated Tankeh like a goat; others that it was far better to eat dust than to swallow grass like a cow being fed for slaughter. Masutu in particular summoned the strength in his voice that was sharp like a spear to say that dust was good food since babies ate it, but that most grasses were poisonous, at which many more teeth were bared, some brown with kolanut remains, some again darkened by the caress of tobacco smoke.

Yeisi was also in this group.

Not tall, not short, just full, she was dark in a clean way, so that looking at her was like looking at the finest gift of nature's work.

They were talking and going along the Nwemba-bank of Mantum, towards the place where the river crashed into a fall. The sound of the falling water rose from down below coloured by thin white sheets of vapour that settled on their heads and gave them the looks of wise men.

At the point where the vapour was thickest, Yeisi tore away from the group and headed back towards the place of the fight. She ran like one running away from a bad thing. But she did not go far. Sendelenghi ordered her back just as she was about to disappear in the bend behind them. She returned quietly but with a strong decision. Sendelenghi again… She knew where he was going with all that but her mind would not be changed.

Sendelenghi stared at her as she came up. The look in his face was hot, and spoke of strong things inside him. She did not give back the look. She only walked up and stood at the edge of the little group, throwing her eyes away towards the fall, at the crashing water that swallowed much of their voices. He cried out:

"Yeisi, come forward."

She threw the orders to the ground and tore off again, back down the road and away beyond the bend. She ran and ran, panting all along, and did not stop until she was in my house.

Lemea was pressing my ribs with sponge and warm water.

"Hyena!" Yeisi panted from the door.

"My sister," Lemea said raising her head.

I only groaned to the aches.

"I don't want to see a fight like this one again," Yeisi said, hitting her shoulders with her two hands in protest; then, catching her breath, added: "Let me do it."

"You have a softer hand," Lemea said, stepping aside to hand the job over to Yeisi. "At least with you he can feel something."

"That's why I climbed on him," I said, fighting away the pain.

52

"For her soft hands on your body," Lemea said.

"Just that."

"Don't mind him," Yeisi said. "When I press his body the other times, is it because he has fought?"

"Ewo! But this one was bad," Lemea cried.

"You say bad? I almost jumped in," Yeisi said. "I was shaking and screaming." She stopped, then looked at me and said softly: "Promise that this will be the last time."

I said no with as much defiance as pain could allow.

"For my sake."

"It is for your sake that I do all this," I said.

"I don't understand," she said.

"Don't waste your time," Lemea interrupted. "I too have pleaded until I'm tired."

"This your fighting will kill some of us before our time," Yeisi said.

"Do they understand? I will only sit here and hear that Tankeh Winjala has killed him." Lemea said. She was holding her head in her two hands.

"He cannot," Yeisi said defiantly, almost jumping to her feet. "Tankeh Winjala cannot do Banda anything. You should have been there to see the fight. This your brother is a tiger."

"I'm tired seeing them," Lemea offered, almost resignedly.

"How can I stay away?" Yeisi wondered, her one hand pinching my jaw, but not hard. "Each time they fight it's like Nwemba will disappear. And that Sendelenghi with his big mouth is always there putting fire on Tankeh's side."

"Any cause has its own supporters," I said.

"I don't know what that one wants from me," Yeisi spat.

"Sendelenghi or Tankeh Wiinjala?" Lemea asked.

"Sendelenghi. He follows me the way a drunkard follows palmwine. I don't know…"

"He has been saying all over the village that you cannot escape him," Lemea said, with a tinge of challenge.

53

"He must be talking about another Yeisi, not this one," Yeisi answered in a voice steady in a way that gave no hint of firmness, but with a face on which it was clearly said that if Nwemba had only Sendelenghi for a man she would prefer to dump herself in Mantum and go down in pieces. "After the fight he carried our group towards the fall and kept shouting and saying how Tankeh Winjala gave Banda dust to eat. But trust Masutu. He gave it back to him."

"Masutu? You cannot beat him when it comes to putting you in your place! He will give it back to you word for word," Lemea said, then questioned, visibly nervously: "How did you find yourself in that group?"

"Masutu. It was Masutu's presence that deceived me. Before I opened my eyes we were already by the fall. That was when I ran away."

"Why did you run away again?" I questioned, grinning with pain. The two girls laughed and fell in each other's arms.

Yeisi rose and held me from behind, allowing her breasts to touch my bare back.

"If it was the sponge you would now be twisting and turning," Lemea teased.

Yeisi giggled, then went towards the door saying in Lemea's direction: "Brother for brother."

"My greetings to him," I said. "Tell him I'm almost through with the work."

"Fight less and work more, Tiger," she said, then ran out into the yard and away.

"I've never known you to deny Yeisi anything," Lemea said as she picked up the sponge and returned to my back.

"Not anything I can give her."

"And this one…the promise…what is so difficult in it?"

I removed her hand from my body before saying: "You are too small to understand."

"Fear, Banda…fear will kill me."

"Soothe my pains and leave the rest to me."

"But for how long?"

"For how long…"

I did not continue. Instead, I pressed my side as if to feel the flow of blood in it, then said: "See Nwemba. Take your head up and see. It has been denied the good things. The big roads have come and remained in Meamba."

"The schools too. I hear one has been opened in Fetet. The children there now talk the white man's talk."

"So you know. And you tell me to stop. How can I? Tankeh Winjala is standing in the way of my second victory, the one that will open the road for the white man. But he shall not have his way."

"Father's whisper?"

"The whisper…that is it. He turned his face towards Meamba and died. How can I forget?"

I felt the sponge leave my back and I turned round to see Lemea standing away from me and looking down on the floor. She raised her eyes, not towards me but in the direction of the open door. Night had come fully so that she could not see in the darkness outside.

"Banda," she called.

I could count the number of times Lemea had called me in this kind of voice.

"Lemea," I answered with fear.

"Meamba reminds me of the drawing in that your book."

"The children in the classroom?"

"Yes, and the little girl showing up her hand."

"I know you liked it very much."

"I would have liked to be like that little girl."

"But father did not want it."

"Do you know why? Or did he think I could not do it?"

"Not that. He said you would learn more and better sitting by mother."

"Did you believe that?"

"No. I used to think how nice it would be if you and I returned from the white man's school together as I saw other boys and their sisters doing."

"That's all I wanted to hear. I'm glad."

The sponge returned to my back and the movement was soft and drove away all the bite of pain.

Chapter Six

The Meamba towards which our father had sent his last gaze lay to the west of Nwemba. Its zinc-roofed houses shone in the bright sun in the day, and in the night its sky twinkled as if lit by flying crowds of fireflies.

But not so Nwemba. With nightfall the village rolled itself up like an over-fed python, so that one had to reach its outer limits and actually touch the houses to notice their being there. The bamboo fires glowed in the early hours of evening, but their glow remained locked in the households, known only to the mothers busy with cooking and to the greyed ones journeying enthralled children into the founding exploits of Nwembwana.

The roads in the village were not big or straight. They were narrow tracks beaten clean by feet. On them one always ended up more or less where one set out for, and since time was in plentiful supply, the paths that wound and twisted like a snake did not bother the villagers at all.

"The fear in you should not be for me," I said again to Lemea. "We have been to Meamba and back. We have seen the white man and his magic. If you have any fear in you, it should be for Nwemba. Winjala the Crude said before dying that the white man's things will never come to Nwemba."

"And our own father on dying said they would."

"That is where I stand. You know that well."

"But you will not buy it with your life."

"My life is in my father's vow."

"Only death can make you change," my sister said in defeat.

It was not long after I went to bed that the noises of the waking village came to my ears with stubborn persistence. I turned over in bed muttering impotently, but still the noises came, ever louder, ever more irritating. I rose lazily and angrily, caught a chewing-stick between my lips and went out into the yard where mother was giving the chicks their morning feed. Some had retired to a corner and were preening themselves, but most of them were still cackling about her, darting and kicking and flapping their wings.

A big red cock emerged from behind the house. I watched it climb without resistance on a hen's back, play a flipping game of balance there and climb down. I watched the hen fluff its feathers in total happiness. The way the cock cackled and lurked, the way the hen offered itself – the whole thing struck me with new meaning and I thought: Why could men not do like those two birds? The ways of men…so wanting in appeal... no invitation, only action, brutal action. The abused women either swallowed the abuse or then dumped themselves in Mantum or tied cloths round their necks and allowed their tongues to hang out. Men kept many women and went from one to the other, filling them with dirt and child, then returned to their huts to laugh their crimes into the air of the village. Many women in the village were survivors in a rat race. Many others had died, claimed by disease or childbirth. That my own mother was still alive I did not know who to thank for: she carried a dead child in her belly for two weeks and discharged it in clotted fragments in the white man's hospital in Meamba …that she was still breathing and on her feet was one of those things for which one only gave thanks. At least my father had done her all the honour a man could do a woman. He had died liking her; just as he had lived liking her. But that was not the way all the men in Nwemba behaved to their wives. Maybe if he hadn't gone to Meamba and seen the white man and his wife, he too would not have been any different. I remembered him saying he had it in mind to marry many other women. That's the way it always started. They married one, then another one, and another one; and soon there were so many of them that the man quite simply lost count, and interest. And then the women started wandering, like cows without a herdsman...

It was only now that mother noticed me and my still chewing stick. She put down the empty calabash bowl in her hand and came midway between our two houses.

"The day has broken," she greeted.

"Thank the gods," I answered before asking how she slept.

"Well, my son. We thank the gods." Her words were a bit lame, as if they had stumbled against a sad happening on their way out. She picked up her calabash bowl again and said backing me as if in maternal protest: "Your sister said you fought again."

"The son of Winjala the Crude tried to drive me away from Mantum."

"My son, leave the banks to him."

"And my second victory?"

"I know your father talked about it, but it must not be."

"It must be, and no later than this season."

"It's your life I fear for."

"Don't fear for my life. Fear for Nwemba."

She did not pursue the exchange. She knew me well enough not to try to pull me out of a position I had taken. My father on dying had said I must free Nwemba from the curse of Winjala the Crude. She knew I would put all I had in me into achieving that aim. She knew it well; that was why she instead went in and brought out her hoe.

"And where is that for?"

"The Chief's farm. We are working on it today."

"Only to return late at night in song. And my stomach?"

"Lemea will cook for you."

"Make sure she knows what to cook before you go."

"I will tell her what to cook, my son," she said, then added with a voice dried of hope: "But think of a wife. Let me carry your child before I die."

"Wife…child…those things will come in their own time."

Just then Lemea came up the path with a big clay pot on her head and her two hands wiping off trickles from her face.

"This way…come this way."

"Is that your morning greeting?" she threw back light-heartedly as she settled the clay pot before me.

"Good morning, breath of my grandmother."

A warm smile lit her face.

"Take some of the water into my house. While I'm washing my face you get something ready for my mouth. I need to take Olembe's carving to him and see Manyi."

"Yeisi told me something," she said in a giggle. "Manyi… it was about her."

"Not about me this time."

"Not you. Manyi…that she is pregnant."

"Nwemba will be free!"

"You did well to hand her to Olembe."

"I could not have left her here. Tankeh Winjala would have poisoned her a long time ago."

"The gods be thanked."

"And my stubbornness too. I must see her this morning."

"Which of the hers?" she asked humorously.

"The pregnant one."

"Look at him!"

We both laughed. I put back the half-filled pot on her head. As she turned to go I heard her say: "I want to see both of them too."

I turned into my house and almost immediately the bleating choir of kids stormed my ears. But I did not see any. I only heard their noises from which I could gather that they were searching for milk. As the noises rose more and more I reached for my stool and dropped myself on it. Soon the bleating merged into chants of victory like on the day Chief Ndelu handed me the prize goats at the end of the first contest.

The sun was high overhead but not piercing: muscles prepared for the contest had to be protected from the bite of the pre-noon sun so that blood did not heat up but flowed at a steady rhythm beneath the skin. It was with this in mind that the Council placed the contest in the part of the year when the sun was more seen than felt.

As I stood watching the Chief water dripped from my head down over my chest and collected above the rolled-up barricade of my loincloth. Then the gong went and the bank grounds became voiceless. Only Yeisi, standing some way off behind the male-drum -beater, opened her mouth to let go a string of wilililis, but the drum-beater's large hand blocked her mouth before they escaped to disrupt the ritual.

At the end of the contest Chief Ndelu spoke facing the sun: "Banda that sprang from the manseed of Sama Gakoh. This day you have won." Yeisi let go the first salve of wililili, then the girls picked up, filling the air with ripples of praise chant. The boys waited for the chant to die down, then they jumped into dance, and danced round and round me, circling a net over my head.

"This year's contest has been good," the Chief resumed after the dance by my age-group. "A good contest like this is also good for the village…"

I remembered all these things, how the Chief handed me the prize goats; how Yeisi jumped and held me and we nearly fell to the ground. I also remembered Tankeh standing at the edge of the crowd and refusing to shake hands with me when everybody else was doing so.

The sustained bleating was now stumbling into isolated noises that one could not attribute to any particular kind of animal. I got up from my stool and posted myself at the door and called out for Lemea, but no answer came back. "These women," I said to myself, then turned back in and reached for Olembe's carving.

As I drew up to Ewinjika's compound I heard Nabu, Ewinjika's daughter by his third wife, cursing flies. Just before the entrance into the compound I stopped and peeped through an opening in the fence to see Nabu in front of her mother's house with her ulcer in the sun and a white cowtail whisk doing battle with the flies. Her eyes searched the fence gate as if in anticipation of a god-sent healer.

I drew my eyes away and doubled my pace like one running away from a past he was ashamed of. As I paced away my head ran its own race into my past, bringing up memories of the things we had done together. It was interesting how I could be running into something while running away from it. Memories of my young days. They crowded more and more into my head, filling me with guilt. Could there be some release in self confession? Poor girl. The gods of Nwemba know I have no hand in this. All I did was say no to the plans. How could I accept a thing my heart spoke against? The day you went to the bush for the mpkete leaves Masutu crossed you on the way and said no don't go. But you insisted. And you ran into a trap meant for bushfowls. So where is my hand in it?

A voice came up the path: "Banda son of Gakoh! Banda...!"

The power of the calling voice stopped me and I turned round to see Masutu running up the road.

"Masutu!"

"I knew I would catch you just here."

"The gods come to my help."

"The village knew the two of you."

"But those were childhood days."

"Childhood things have been known to survive into manhood things."

"But not this time."

"Foolish little thing," Masutu let out. "I said she should not go to the bush, but would she hear? Our people say the day you will meet trouble you leave your father's house with a run."

"I feel bad."

"You don't need to. At her small age she wanted to charm a man. Mpkete leaves. bad leaves. A bushfowl trap was planted right in the shrub and she walked into it."

"And to think that the trap was set by her own father."

The sky clapped and rumbled and before we knew what was happening we were caught in the thick of a sudden storm. I caught Masutu's hand and dragged him towards the tree with its tip nipped as by a tapping machete.

"No! Not there!" Masutu screamed. "Thunder...back...let's run back to Ewinjika's compound." At this he broke off towards Ewinjika's house which lay some distance downhill. I let him go and continued forward in the direction of Olembe's house, inside my brooding. Marriage was for you a thing of life or death. Those mpkete leaves would have charmed me but would they have sealed a good marriage between us?

The voice again. "Banda son of Gakoh! Banda...!"

I turned and saw Masutu coming back up the path with his head buried inside a flapping plantain leaf. "You are continuing like this that where am I?"

"How did you think I would seek shelter in Ewinjika's house?"

"Never mind. Only I turned and never saw you."

"Throw your leaf. The rain has ceased."

Masutu threw away the plantain leaf and we looked at each other and burst into laughter.

"I want Lemea to see you this way," I said humorously.

"Laikum forbid. She told me you were on your way to visit Olembe."

"And yet when I was leaving I called and she refused to answer."

"She answered but you did not hear."

"The devil's advocate."

"The friend's mouthpiece. But let that pass. Yesterday after the fight Sendelenghi took us towards the fall. I thought I should let you know."

"Yeisi told me yesterday."

"Yes she was with us. I even forgot."

"What is he hunting the fall for?"

"Why? How can you ask such a question? The second contest."

"And so they think that by spoiling the fall they will stop me from winning the contest?"

"That and other things."

"Other things?"

"Like your marriage. Are you not going to visit Yeisi?"

"Yes, but also to take Olembe's carving to him."

"Sendelenghi has put his foot on the ground. Tankeh Winjala has put his foot on the ground. Sendelenghi says you will not marry Yeisi. Tankeh son of Winjala the Crude says you will not win the second contest."

"So if I cannot marry Yeisi and cannot win the second contest, then what am I good for? What do they say I should do with myself? Jump into Mantum? Become their footstool?"

"It is always good that when these things are said they should be known. Go where you are going. I will return to my house."

"Did you leave that girl at home?"

"She was fastening her cloth and saying she would reach Olembe's house before you."

"But how? This is the road."

"She talked of the one by the dried-up pond."

"I don't like that road and I have told her so. Go back there quickly and tell her not to take that road. I know those are the kinds of errands you like."

"As if you are not on your own."

Masutu turned and ran down the path towards our house. I stood and watched the speed with which he disappeared. It was as though he was flying. That's the way it is when your heart is light. Not only my message put that speed in his legs. He had his own things to tell Lemea: things of the heart. It was those things that made his feet light, that put the speed of a man deer in them.

As Masutu disappeared I continued on my own road. I had now gone some distance from Ewinjika's compound, but Nabu's image continued to dance in my mind and to remind me of many many things I was not happy to recall... You saw only the way we were happy...but we were still small. Your eyes were on the ground but my own were up looking at the days to come, when we become big. I too could have said yes, but I did not want a thing that brought only worry. That was the reason for my no. But in answer you went for mpkete leaves and returned with the mouth of a bushfowl trap in your leg. Both of us were strangers to what they said... heavy things were decided for us, heavy things that our shoulders were too small to carry. See our noses. We could not even clean the dirt from them. But that did not matter. We were man and wife, they said... I was the man, you the woman. We used to sit together and lick our running noses, and I always enjoyed doing it with you. Wasn't it always me who ran away from home with my dirty belly and came to you? But when the dirt from our noses went away I stopped coming. I did not like your face after that. So I stopped coming. But our parents had forgotten that one day I would look at your face..."

I raised my head and saw Olembe leaning against his door.

"My eyes have been on the road since daybreak," he said, before asking: "Were you swimming in Mantum?"

"A storm. I ran into a storm shortly after Ewinjika's compound. I see it didn't get here."

"You would have seen it on the ground. Come. You can't remain in these clothes. I'll get you a cloth and singlet." As he said this he entered his room and came out with a broad piece of blue cloth and a netlike singlet. "Get into these quickly before you are seen."

"Let them only see me like this. Then they will know how much we suffer for them."

"They don't think like that. They will laugh at you instead."

"You are a better mind in these things."

"At least I have been in them longer than you!"

I changed into the cloth and singlet and Olembe poured me a cowhornfull.

"That's some wine. And where are they?"

"Leave them out of this first. Yesterday's fight….where did it come from?"

"Once you hear Mantum you understand. The son of Winjala the Crude follows me everywhere. This time he said I was by the bank to spoil the spot he had chosen for his net at the next contest."

"Isn't that a child's thing to say?"

"That's all he knows. I was by the bank, it's true."

"But is the bank forbidden? Does anyone stop him from going there?"

"I wonder. When he provoked me I was at my own place and he was at his own. But he left his own place and came over to me and in no time he was in between my legs."

"So he was the one who attacked you."

"You know I will not provoke a fight. Not with Tankeh Winjala for any reason."

"But that's not what Sendelenghi said. I reached the place late. Sendelenghi kept saying it was you who attacked Tankeh first because your belly was turning."

"Me, my belly turning. I can fish anywhere in that river, even down in the fall and will still take fish from the running water. I will beat Tankeh Winjala flat at the next contest. Both of them know that. Sendelenghi should look for an image for himself instead of leaning on a rotten trunk."

"He continues to say all kinds of things about my sister."

"Don't trouble yourself with that. She can take care of herself very well."

"I see she can," Olembe said in a rich laughter. "She told me how she pressed your body yesterday after the fight and you kept screaming like a baby. Baby tiger, that's what she calls you."

"I was glad she came. I was in serious pains."

"Can you believe that Sendelenghi lured her to the place where the fall is deepest?"

"And what does he think he can get out of her?"

"Nothing."

We broke into laughter. Olembe cut his own laughter short and turned to the object in his hand. "What craftsmanship!"

"Oh well, when you have a model such as I had, the object comes alive. When the model is present in you, in your hands, in your mind, shaping the figure becomes like bringing her out of the wood. You open the door in the wood and she comes out. It is like digging up a treasure. By the way, where is she?"

"Yeisi!" Olembe called in the direction of the little hut where they cooked.

"Why don't the two of you just leave me alone?" came the answer in a voice like that of a little bird.

"Come and see what I'm seeing," I invited teasingly though with little success.

"I'm not coming, even if it's a life deer."

"Alright. I'll bring it to you myself," I thundered, rising and flipping my cloth into place.

"Are these your eyes I'm seeing?" Yeisi queried, collecting her skirt into her laps. Smoke danced in her hair and made her look like a woman with four children. Only her full breasts and her smooth black skin denied her the joys of motherhood.

"Where is the deer?"

"This is it standing before you," I said in laughter.

"Maybe you think you're such a man. Go and show yourself elsewhere," she said, turning her head away sharply. "There are many girls in Nwemba, so just leave me alone."

"Tell me where to find them."

"Who are you trying to fool? You sniff the air of this village like a starving wolf. What about Nabu, eh? You just tell me. Did her father not drink your palm-wine? Have you not been covering her with bangles and expensive cloth? Go where the good things are and leave me alone." As she said this she poked the fire so hard that flying sparks caught me in the chest. I jumped backward but returned to my position almost immediately.

"I've never given Nabu anything. You know that yourself," I protested. "As for my palm-wine, why stop people from coming to my house and drinking palm-wine? I never carried palm-wine to Nabu's father. You know that."

"Was it not because of you that she went for mpkete leaves and sold her leg to a bushfowl trap?"

"I leave you to answer that for me. Mpkete leaves are bad leaves."

"You alone know what you have done to her. Only know that I will never lose my leg for anybody."

"That's a good thing to hear. I want those legs kept whole."

"You will not tell me what to do with my legs."

"No, but I can say how I like them."

"They are not yours as far as I know."

"Not yet."

"Banda, I've told you to leave me alone and return to your palm-wine. Is that not what brought you here?"

"Yes, palm-wine. Olembe's palm-wine, and some other palm-wine too, the special one I sip with mother. And where is she, if I may ask?"

"You know where to find her fireplace. As for the wine you sip with her, its dregs will stick in your throat like crayfish-bone. But before you go where you are going, I want to tell you something, if you care to listen."

I became ready for one of those games of go but stay.

"It's not my place to say these things, but I cannot pretend not to know them, or swallow them with water."

"Ah, I see mother has been opening the bag to you each time I drop something in it."

"The secrets you trade with my mother don't worry me. Camwood will not refuse marriage with my skin because of you and my mother. Tankeh. It's about him."

My chest started to dance.

"We farm the land behind his palm-wine bush, remember? I was there yesterday to harvest the plantains you see there, and I saw him."

Anxiety threw me into the smoke-filled kitchen before I knew I was inside. I looked into Yeisi's face but nothing more was coming. Instead, she bent her head to one side and blew the fire into flames.

"Tankeh...what about him?"

"He called your name," she said, straightening up. "...you and Dinga."

"Dinga ...Dinga?"

"He was repeating your names again and again and spraying palmwine into the air. Your name jumped from his mouth several times, but Dinga's only a few times."

"Yeisi, Tankeh's magic will not work on me." I turned and faced the door, then added: "I'm returning to my wine."

"Not yet," she pressed on. "Lemea. He also called her name. I don't know what's in all this, but I thought you should know."

"Lemea, Dinga and me in Tankeh's mouth. What really can there be in all this?"

"Only the coming days will tell. But now that I have told you, don't ever say you did not know."

"Can I now go?"

"Don't only go. Run. Drunkard baby tiger."

I stormed out.

"I feel cheated," Olembe protested, inattentive to the troubled look on my face.

I said I was sorry. That Olembe did not see the look on my face helped to kill the worrying things Yeisi had just told me.

The smell of hot ngeng with bonsuh in ngwet-ban filled the room. I clapped my lips and threw a warm look at Olembe whose nose too was dancing and twitching.

Yeisi burst into view, her head bent away from the rising flavour. I smiled a big smile into Olembe's face. He returned it with a mixed look of pride and jealousy, jealousy of a happy kind, a jealous happiness. But the proud look soon ate the jealous look, so that as Yeisi placed the food on the floor a new happiness seemed to whip up our appetite.

"There's no meat in it," she said, half in apology, half in defiance.

"Meat? Who wants meat anyway?" I laughed. "Besides, you'll never lack meat when we share the same roof."

"Banda, maybe your ears are overgrown with deaf-grass. Your roof is for you. Don't you think I'm so interested in it. I'm not and never will be."

"You…you…" I stopped midway into the effort to clean the oil running down the left corner of my mouth. "Oh, what was I trying to say? This food here!... it just kills my thinking. Yeisi you will never lack meat…no… nor oil… nor ogbono… nor …"

70

"She's back in the kitchen," Olembe cut in, "so wash down the rest of the talk with palm-wine."

"Pour me a cowhorn, a good one…fill it…pour to the brim…let the cool wine caress my flesh. Food like this must be celebrated…and so must the hands that prepared it."

While I was engaged like this in praise a goat passed outside. Its shadow fell across the door in such thick shapes that one would have taken them for other goats.

"A goat has just passed," I said in my friend's direction.

"Manyi," Olembe said. "She is doing her second round, the one that takes the sun to bed."

"Symbol of hope," I cried in a tone that surprised Olembe with its happiness.

"Symbol of hope," he echoed, then leaned backwards on his chair, spilling cup in hand.

I leant forward and took a long draw. The palmwine was only slightly hard. One could drink many cups of such wine and still know the road home. At this time of its journey to hardness, palmwine was even known to help the head more, the more it was taken. It made one talk faster and clearer, made laughter louder and longer, tears – when they came – hot and fast. In such times palmwine was not just palmwine: it was the man in man, the tears in woman; it was the laughter and the wililili, the nights without sleep. More than anything else, it was talk given action.

Olembe tapped more than he drank. The real drinker between us was me, but this time I had touched him with my calabash virus so that his words were now fast and pressing, words of action, not just of wish.

"Exile hangs over your head if you lose the next contest," he said from his reclining position. "But I am confident. The river spirits help those who help themselves. I know you will do everything to win… to win for Manyi. You can. I may even stay out of it. I don't see the point entering if victory will only bring me sorrow."

"You can't stay out. If victory is mine I will have it. I hear Tankeh Winjala is invoking my name everyday."

"He has won the contest once before. If he wins it again his father's wish will inherit Nwemba."

"The contest of light."

"The contest of light. He calls it *bet njen.*"

"Bet njen...."

"Bet njen...the contest of darkness. But I fear. Like all the winners before him he sacrificed his own victory goats to Mantum. So he can rely on the river spirits. No winner before you ever did what you did. You ignored the river spirits in victory."

"I know I have broken the laws of our people."

"A grave thing to do."

"But where have those laws taken us?"

"Why, are you not a son of this village?"

The question remained in my head for some time. Are you not a son of this village? Yet Olembe was not present with us when the white man spoke to me in Meamba. Or was his spirit there with us? The white man said I should return to my village where I would be more useful. It's as if Olembe was with us in spirit on that day because here he was asking me if I was not a son of this village. Again I saw the white man and his words, his white hand on my head and him telling my father to take me back to the village, that he could have kept me with him in Meamba and later send me to another school in his country, but he had dropped all that so my father could take me back to our village. These people saw far. How could he see standing in Meamba that many moons after we returned to Nwemba, Olembe would ask me if I was not a child of the village? How could he see that? My father used to say these white people were medicine men. Is this what he meant? Only a medicine man, a man with nine eyes, could see a happening many, many moons before it came.

Take even how he and his wife came to be with us. Where was their own country? How did they know that they could travel like this and like this and come to a place called Ediki-Mbeng? I could not remember the number of times I got missing on the way the first time I went to Tazim. Tazim is just half a day's walk from Nwemba, but I missed my way many times, branching into villages that lay long distances out of the right road. How did this white man and his wife do it without getting missing like me on the way to Tazim? Were these not the kinds of things only medicine men did? And Winjala the Crude wanted to turn this power away from Nwemba.

"See Meamba," I said. "At least you have been there. I have lived there and gone to the white man's school. My father was a cook to Pete Harrington. See Meamba…see it at night. Night there is like day."

But Olembe refused to see. "*Here* is what we are talking about," he threw at me.

"There can be no here without a there," I said.

"That's for you to say," he threw back. "It is here that I want us to look at. The spirits…they are in command."

"In this your *here* only," I said, pressing emphatically on the 'here' with a smile that bent somewhat at the edge.

"But are they not?" Olembe said, rising sharply to what he saw as a wrong attack on the gods. "Or are you underrating them?"

I offered no answer.

"I'm sorry I brought all this up." There was apology in the voice with which he said this, but not the kind of apology that came from guilt, such as when you betrayed a secret or hurt an affection. It was just as if he wanted to see the exchange end.

"You did well," I reassured him. "Manyi and I need to be reminded now and again that we are still in harm's way."

I threw my right hand at the little hut, then said to Olembe: "Tell her she can now leave the kitchen."

"You can stay there for the next ten moons," we heard from the direction of the kitchen.

As I turned to go I saw Manyi returning from her second round. I stopped to touch her but she carried her heavy self away instead.

I stood watching her go, thinking all the time of the battle that had opposed me to the village over her. I thought of the trials, how everyone had wanted me to kill her. Villagers would sit in small groups under this tree or that, around a calabash of palmwine, and put Manyi and me before them for discussion.

"That son of Gakoh."

"I hear the goat is even pregnant."

"Who ever heard such a thing?"

"And the gods, where are they?"

"They will talk…when their time comes."

"Every day that passes makes their anger bigger."

The minds of the villagers were held by fear of what would come from the gods. And they asked many questions. Why were the gods not talking? Why had I not yet been cut down? Was it that the gods were not seeing? Or were they blinded by anger?

After my victory in the previous year's contest, I had sacrificed only one of my prize goats, the male one, to Mantum in thanksgiving. Tradition required that I sacrifice all two. But I turned my back on that tradition, wilfully, suicidally even; yes, suicidally. This was an affront unknown to the gods. No winner had ever spared the life of a goat that rewarded his victory. Immediately following the contest, the winner gathered the village in a solemn occasion of thanksgiving and with the Chief's blessing sacrificed both goats to Mantum, home of the spirits, holders and givers of fish. It was a permanent belief that no-one could win the fishing contest against Mantum's wish. The double sacrifice was therefore not only of thanksgiving; it was also an expression of hope that the river spirits would in the coming

74

season repeat their graces. The truth is that no one person had ever won the contest twice in succession. In fact, no-one had ever won it two times.

Yes, the gods decided the outcome of each contest. Mantum's deities held all its life matter in absolute fealty, disposing of them in a manner and for reasons known only to them. Fish did not enter a net until a god had put it there. Which fish in which net, why and when were strands of the divine ordering into which men peeped only with awe. Man never beat his chest…was never allowed to do so…never dared to do so in victory… victory that came from the gods…victory that was held only in fleeting enjoyment and celebration by man before it was returned to the gods in the form of the double sacrifice.

You did not fly in the face of this time-old order and still remained alive to celebrate your bravado. Many voices had therefore risen in disapproval of my insult to the river spirits. Who was I to kick tradition like that in the face? I would pay, unfailingly, many had predicted. Chief Ndelu had even summoned me to his palace late one night and ordered me to offer Manyi as well to Mantum or face exile if I lost the next contest. But I had stood my ground, preferring instead to place Manyi in Olembe's care. Now she was pregnant. And more and more I remembered that she was called Manyi.

A new urge filled me to see her again. Would she come back, or had she retired for the night? Although she had disappeared behind Olembe's house I maintained the faith that something would cause her to reappear. I now wondered why I had not looked for her as soon as I arrived even though she was one of the reasons why I came. Yeisi. She was the one with her Tankeh and Dinga stories mingled with accusations of gifts I never made to Nabu. Where did she get her own information from? And how could she claim ignorance of the bad ulcer in the girl's leg? She only wanted to press home her trumped-up charge and fill me with guilt feelings she knew I did not deserve.

If she had not distracted me with her little worries, maybe I would have looked for Manyi immediately upon arrival and taken a better look at her in her new condition. From the little I saw, the pregnancy was still in its early stages; but her belly was starting to swing just a bit from side to side in rhythmic obedience to her maternal condition.

When it became clear that I would not see her again for that day, I pulled myself away towards my house. Once again, Nabu came back into my head, and with her the gnawing question: had I done all I could to help? Was it enough for me to pass on my way to Olembe now and again and express sadness at a condition I was directly responsible for?

A certain feeling of helplessness seized hold of me in all this brooding. Maybe if this happening had occurred in Meamba I would have been in a position to act more decisively.

Meamba and Ediki-Mbeng had revealed things to me the rest of Nwemba did not know. For example, none of them knew that if you fell in a trap and you were carried to the white man's medicine house they did not throw cowries on the ground or cover your leg in weeds. They pierced your buttock with a sharp needle that caused your wound to dry quickly and nicely.

Each time I went past Ewinjika's compound and saw Nabu drying her bad wound in the sun my mind went back to Meamba and to the many things the medicine house there would have done.

The very day she was carried back from the bush with her leg eaten by a bushfowl trap, I would have put her on a bicycle – that was another one Nwemba did not know – and taken her to the medicine house. In Meamba it was called a hospital. I would have put her on a bicycle and taken her to the hospital. As soon as the people there saw me they would have rushed out and helped me to carry her into their house and put her on a long table before asking her a string of questions…no…not a string of questions.

That was not how they started. They would have given her something to stop the pains first, then ask her what happened. They had a special language in which to ask these questions, and a special way too that they used even in such details as touching the wounded one on the long table.

It was hard not to want to be like them when you saw how they talked, the nice quiet way they put their questions so that no matter the pains you still found the courageous pleasure in you to tell them what happened. The thought of being like them had entered my mind and stayed there for a long time, until the white man sent word to me in Ediki Mbeng to say I should return to Meamba because I was soon to go back to Nwemba with my family. Maybe if it had been my own father who sent me to Ediki Mbeng, I would be one of those people in that hospital receiving wounded people like Nabu and touching their wounds the special way we were taught to do it. I did not feel any bitterness when the white man called me back to Meamba; I only felt sad that his kindness to me was brought to such a sudden end.

The day Nabu fell in a bushfowl trap she lay there in the shrub bleeding and shouting at the top of her voice the whole day with the trap fangs buried deep in her leg. It was only late in the evening that women returning from the Chief's farm heard a loud noise and sped there and discovered her. By now the trap had eaten deep and its teeth refused to come off without chunks of flesh.

The women had spent the whole day tilling the Chief's farm so they were themselves tired. All they could do was help her to limp along until she got home. Then she was left there under her mother's care. What could the old woman do? Everyday she applied a bit of palmoil to the wound and offered her shoulder to her daughter to hang on and limp to the yard to start the day's battle with flies. Now she was rearing an ulcer.

Ulcer. Bad wound. I felt Nabu's pains, every drop of it, even more than if the wound had been on my own leg. The pain was not only on my skin. It was more in my blood. That of all the girls in Nwemba it should be Nabu to suffer this kind of torment was something I could not find the strength in me to accept. There were some legs that were not made for wounds. Even in our very young days when we used to meet with running noses, my eyes never left Nabu's legs. Some women are made beautiful by just one part of their body. Nabu's was her legs. They made her gracious; they gave her a compelling power of attraction. Now it was just as if that bushfowl trap had bitten into my own flesh. Which I wouldn't have minded, especially with Meamba in my life.

A wound had been cut in my leg too, as a schoolchild in Meamba. I'd been building the compost pit and had stood on a broken bottle, receiving the sharp end of the thing deep in my right heel so that I could only limp out of the pit and throw myself on the ground nearby before opening my mouth to a scream. I imagined what would have happened to me if this accident had occurred in Nwemba. I too would be sitting in the sun in front of my mother's house and fighting with the flies. Maybe the leg would even have rotted so badly that it would have fallen off, as Nabu's was threatening to do. I shivered at the thought.

It was Harrington that had brought the hospital to Meamba. He had brought many other things as well, but what the people of Meamba talked most about was the hospital. I was almost tempted to write to him. He had said I could if I encountered any difficulty. Nabu's leg was a difficulty. Should I write or leave Nabu's leg to fall off? I thought about this for long. I could invite him to come with one or two people from his hospital. I still had some unused exercise books and one or two pens. Somebody would have to take the letter to him in Meamba. It was two days' trek, but that could be done. A fast person could even use a day and a night. Could Masutu do it? If I promised him Lemea he would, happily. I liked him as a friend and I wouldn't mind having him as a brother-in-law. This is something he had waited for me to say ever since, but I had always held back. Lemea loved him. I could tell that in the warmth of her voice each time she talked about him. I could make my acceptance a reward for his errand to the white man in Meamba. Ough! Whatever I thought regarding Lemea still had to pass Uncle Abua's test; all the same, I could still go ahead and tell Masutu that I was for his marrying my sister, and then send him on an errand to Meamba with a letter for the white man.

The only problem was he had never been to that place. He would not know his way around once he got there. There were many stories of people from Nwemba having lost their way in Meamba. He may get there and add to the list of such people. Olembe had been there but he was one person who would not do an errand for anybody. I knew my friend too well. All the same, I would write and look for some way of getting the letter to the white man in Meamba.

But the more I thought of it the more I found it necessary to take my time. The letter I was going to write was just one bullet. If I used it to shoot a small bird and then a lion or even an elephant showed up, I would not be able to face it. I therefore had to be careful and use my bullet only when I knew the time to be ripe for me to do so. There were many challenges ahead. I was entering a time when there was no certainty about what lay ahead. Tankeh, Sendelenghi, the contest, anything could happen that required the white man's presence. Nabu's leg was quite an emergency, but I was not going to use my lone bullet on it. Not with the contest still unresolved. What if I lost it? Winjala the Crude's wish would take hold of Nwemba. Could I still write to the white man under such circumstances? Yes. The answer was yes. I was not going to sacrifice Nabu's leg. Only the white man could save it. Spell for spell. Whether in victory or in defeat, the white man had to come to Nwemba.

Chapter Seven

Tankeh stood by the pond with his back to the path, his broad shoulders arched stiffly forward into a muscular crescent. His gaze, alert and strong as usual, was fixed on a crimson barbet that lay panting faintly, half-buried in the mud just within reach in the dried-up pond.

The brief thud of a trap closing on a catch, then the wild, anguished flapping of wings, had drawn his gaze and he had watched the mud-trapped bird through its struggle to this moment of resigned acceptance.

He shot out his right hand and seized the bird by the neck. It flipped its head in a sudden sideways jerk and its beak parted to a stifled squeak.

He did not drop the bird immediately it died; he continued to hold it firmly in his hand, feeling its cold limbs as if thrilled by the sudden drama of death. Or did he not see death in the open beak? And if he did, was it that he thought the bird's still limbs would come alive again with movement? Strange way to think seeing how the dead bird was buried in his big fingers. Where was the life to come from again? How was it to pass back through a twined neck?

Pleased with himself, he dropped the dead bird, then stretched out his both hands and buried them in the mud and kept them there even as his father stood again before him repeating the command…You must win the next fishing contest. The white man has journeyed close to our house. He is already in Meamba and Fetet. Let him remain there. He must not come to Nwemba. Never.

The night rang with his return promise: Father, I have heard you.

81

As he sent back the answer his buried hands ground the mud in the dried-up pond. The reply was short, but all the power he had in him was put in it. He seemed to have been looking for this meeting with his father, waiting for it. Since the man's death he had waited for something by way of encouragement, anything that would sustain his father's parting assignment to him. Now he had it. The spirit was stronger than the flesh. What the flesh had said the spirit had repeated. And when the two said the same thing, the spirit the same thing as the flesh, there was no other road.

Not that he ever doubted his father's judgment. He had seen the way Nwemba received his words when they returned from Meamba. No-one laughed at him for cutting grass in the white man's house. Every man he talked to agreed that cutting grass was a good thing; after all they cut grass on their own farms before their women worked them. The meeting houses he attended stood behind him to condemn what the white man did to the men of Meamba. They joined him to say the white man in a kaba used bad medicine on the men of Meamba in that his ngomba house where he shouted and raised his hands up and talked with people only he saw. That was not all. He gave them something to eat that made them sleepy for a short time. How could men eat with their eyes closed? If this was not bad medicine, what was it? It was in that moment when they closed their eyes that their manhood was taken away from them and they became women. Once they ate with their eyes closed, they could no longer say no to the white man. Everything he said was right; everything he did was correct. People could not live like that, putting their village in the hands of strangers from far away, even becoming themselves strangers in their own land. His father was right to say this and the villagers joined him in the view that it was wrong for people to live separated from their will, like a hunter from his gun.

Since his father died he had lived with one eye and one ear in the night, looking and listening for when the dead man would come again and repeat his injunction. Not that he doubted the power of the primitive will; it would just have been so much better, so much more reassuring if his father had reiterated the injunction in a sign, a word, a whisper. Fighting a force as strong as the white man's required more than just one statement of will. He may not have said it, but the white man he saw in Meamba you did not just get up one day and say don't come and he did not come. For your will to have any effect, you needed the full backing of the gods, the sustaining drive of the ancestors. If they slept or showed themselves to be sluggish or halfhearted in their support, too bad – they left the doors of the village wide open for the white man to move in. Even when the needed support was given, there was sill no shortage of resolve in the white man to push you and your ancestral army aside and take proud control, as he had done in Fetet.

He removed his hands from the mud where they had remained buried, and wiped them on the dead grass by the pond. The wind was still about. It was no longer strong. It just lingered about lazily, tired by many hours of sustained effort. He retied his lightning-streaked damask cloth and returned to the path leading into Nwemba.

Tall grass settled in thick bushes over the path so that one had to lift it and throw it sideways to make a passage. This was a track not many people used; much less in the night. Only people running away from something they had done, or then those not wanting to be seen, chose it.

He picked his way through the bushy path, not lifting a single stem, not even brushing aside the stray undergrowth of nettle.

Out of the bush part of the path he stopped to pick nettle pins from his cloth and to smooth his itching body.

Footsteps came to his ears. Then a figure appeared.

Though it was still some distance off, he could make out the long slim arms, the quiet steps. The itching melted as if ordered away, and with a nod he continued up the path, his muscular arms beating the air with arrogant power. The weak rays of the sun travelling to Meamba gave his face a borrowed gentleness.

The eyes of the approaching figure misted over as she raised her head. Her feet weakened. She looked behind her but only saw the sun as it dipped behind the hills of Meamba. A choking sensation overcame her. She caught her throat and gasped for breath. One mind said she should turn and race back in the opposite direction. Another mind urged her to throw herself in the elephant grass bush and run in any direction.

She did neither of them but continued forward, gently, as if in a waking nightmare.

Abreast of him she made to pass but a barrier of taut muscles checked her effort. She sank to her knees, struck by fear, but also animated by another feeling she could not immediately tell. His big fingers crackled over her head. She looked up as if to apologize for crossing his path; looked up to beg for his forgiveness.

She opened her mouth to speak but fear killed her voice. She fell to her knees and seized both his ankles the way a man having done wrong would fall before the gods. Foteh, Laikum, Belahmandji…her father had talked to her often about these gods. She would call them to her rescue. So it was not his ankles she was holding but the ankles of the gods. They could not but come to her aid, make her strong, put the right words in her mouth, show her the road away from the agony towering over her.

He tried to work his legs free but in vain. Her grip on them was firm. He felt a strength in the grip that was not human; nothing like say the desperate hold of a drowning man on a feeble branch. The grip was the grip of the gods, strong in a way that no human agency could untie.

The sun hadn't gone down completely. It could still be seen sitting on the flat top of the hill wedged against the horizon towards Meamba. But any moment soon it would tip over, as if pushed below by the coming darkness.

He gave up trying to ply his ankles loose, and spoke in a steady voice that gave the lie to the fears in the kneeling figure.

"It's me Tankeh Winjala. The sun has sought its bed, but when was darkness known to change the face of a friend?"

The girl's hands weakened and fell away from his ankles. He bent and raised her by the arms and she stood in front of him listening to the strange music in her head. She had readied herself for a different language, for harsh words and dirty acts, words and acts that cut deep into her flesh, acts especially that seared her innocence with the flame of lust. She opened her eyes as if out of a dream. Here was a new Tankeh, not the Tankeh she knew. The Tankeh she knew spoke a different language. That Tankeh swore by blood; this one here spoke the language of friendship. Or had she not heard correctly? Hadn't he said darkness does not change the face of a friend? So Tankeh knew the language of friendship. Or were the words meant as a joke on her, a cruel trick to take her in? Whatever the case, a god must have visited this new language on him. Tankeh Winjala, son of Winjala the Crude, was not the kind to blaspheme against the language of his forefathers. This man standing before her and speaking kind words in the night could not be Tankeh Winjala, unless the gods had worked some magic on him. She bared her palms upward.

"You are not saying anything," he said in a half whisper. "Are you afraid? Of me, perhaps?" As he asked this question he wondered in his mind how quickly the little girl had grown…the little girl who survived on caterpillars because her mother's breast milk would not flow.

"Tankeh, there's no fear in me." The words came not from deep inside, where fear gnawed. They spurted from her lips and died before she was aware of having uttered them. But she had found her voice and would wrap her fear in it: "My heart is calm. Didn't you say darkness does not change the face of a friend? Why should I be afraid of a friend?"

"What we call darkness is only a blanket," he droned. His voice was closer to her ears, and so was his breath to hers.

"Tankeh," she said, stepping back silently, "I'm still far away from our compound and it's very dark already."

"A man is by your side. There is no dark night that does not respect men. I will see you home. I will walk you back to your mother's house. I wanted to share a cup with Djitum, but that can wait." His voice had closed in again so that she could catch the warm tremor in it.

"The path home is safe, if I can go now," she pressed on, edging away nervously.

"The path is not in this." The tremor was beginning to stiffen.

"So what do you want me to do?" she asked. The sympathy in her voice unsettled him considerably and caused a brief silence to fall between them. The smell of blood rose to fill the silence. It was an innocent smell, neither acrid nor rough. It was not a fetid smell but a smell rich with the arresting freshness of a crime just committed, a smell whose smell was one with the innocence of the victim.

The silence fell to the ground.

"You treat my invitations like rotten eggs."

"I've always answered your messages, Tankeh, but not the way you wanted me to answer them. You talk like a stranger, as if you do not know how these things are." She fell silent and the confused chant of frogs filled her ears. This talk of invitations sounded like the Tankeh she knew, and thoughts she had tried to subdue returned, crippling in their acuteness. You called Sema and she came. Not a month went by and you called Adisa. Adisa too came. Sema tied a cloth round her neck on the day of her marriage. Adisa was found floating on Mantum.

The light of the pale moon fell just short of her face but Tankeh caught the hidden movement of her loincloth-tip as it rose to the corners of her eyes. She was trembling. Tankeh drew closer and held her. She offered no resistance. The tears of repentance, he thought.

"I'm no stranger in these things," he whispered, tightening his hold slightly. "I want you to come. I want you, tomorrow, after the dance."

"Tomorrow," she repeated, as if in a trance, "yes, I will."

The night had now engulfed both speakers.

She waited, hoping that the grip would loosen, but it didn't. She was beginning to sweat, and nausea too was fast coming. She pressed her thighs together to stop water from running down. Her body was going numb in places, especially where the grip was firmest.

Tankeh's stillness was like that of a lion before the leap. His whole energy was concentrated in that moment and its temptations.

"Can I go now?" She dared.

The noise startled him.

"Can I go now?" she repeated.

"Go? Go." he said, his voice quivering in the night.

She felt the grip drop, like scales from her eyes. The pressing urge returned. She stooped on the spot and the water ran speedily forward, burning her inner ankles.

Some of the gushing hot water pattered on his legs but he did not move aside or utter a complaint. It was as if he was being washed.

She did not wait for her bowels to empty completely but rose as soon as she felt some relief and made to feel her way towards home. Almost instantly he held her again with a grip that was firm as the first time, but no longer choking;

a grip in which a new sensation of warmth and care seemed to vibrate. She tried to break loose but felt somehow that even her body resisted the effort. She just stood there, held by him, waiting, not resignedly, but with some kind of willingness that she herself could not account for.

"Lemea," he said after a long instant.

"Yes, Tankeh," she replied.

"You liked me in Meamba."

The words sounded good, even true, though surprising. How did he know? While they were growing up in Meamba the hostility between their families never gave the two of them room to meet and talk. She liked the way he wrestled, the way he threw the boys, especially Njitifuh. She remembered the many times she hid behind their small family kitchen to watch him defeat this boy or that. Those moments had made her happy and the happiness had shown in the way she washed the pots and pans. Now she laughed in the dark. The knock on her head from Banda ...all that she remembered. But how did he know? He wasn't even asking her whether she liked him. He was saying she did, and with the certainty of someone who held the truth in his hands.

"And you?"

"I liked you too. And I've not stopped. Come. I'll lead you home."

"No, don't," she pleaded. "Banda. If he sees us together he will kill me."

"No fear. I will not let it happen. I will hide in the dark until you have entered your mother's house."

"I'm dying with fear."

"Not anymore."

He led the way and she followed.

Chapter Eight

My door creaked open and a shadow crept in. I didn't raise my head as the light footsteps made the effort unnecessary.

"Where are you from at this time of night?" I questioned as I continued to oil the figure I was on.

"Ma-Nina sent for me. Nina is…"

"Not that name," I said sharply, my attention still taken up by the work in my hand. I looked sideways at her, across the quivering flames of the bamboo fire.

"Banda, please, you know I never leave our compound without a good reason."

"Did Masutu meet you here today?"

She fell silent for a while before offering reluctantly: "Yes."

"And what did you tell him?"

"Banda, please!"

"This is not about Banda."

"I knew that if I followed you to Olembe's house you would drive me away. But I still went there, after you, then I went to Nina."

"You don't want me to believe that Ma-Nina and her daughter kept you for so long. Look outside. The fireflies are lighting the grass."

"She…they…Banda, please." Her eyes were fixed on the ceiling and its black soot.

"You are still to talk." I fell silent. Between us the fire breathed out dancing tongues. I was done with the oiling but didn't put the work away. I held it tightly in my hands and the feel of it sent a warm sensation into my head. The figure was no longer just wood. A fetching look animated its eyes. I could almost feel the thump-thump of its heart. The sensation was such now that even the still plaits tickled my hands. I roamed my sweating fingers through them, listening for a whisper of contentment, a groan of protest, of delight. There was a heart in it. I had felt it beat against mine, sending me off to sleep in the comfort of their unified throb.

"You are still to talk," I said again. "Uncle Abua is in mother's house, so get ready to face him when you get there."

"Banda, please," she pleaded, jumping to me and holding me by the hand, "I heard his voice there. That's why I fled here instead."

"And you think it's here that he will not reach you?"

Just then the door flew open and Uncle Abua stormed in. Contrary to his habit of muttering to himself when in a rage, he had marched the short distance in total silence. Only the sudden bang of the door against the wall had announced his presence.

Lemea sat transfixed on the stool. Her head heaved, as if pounded by waves. The sight of Uncle Abua always dried her blood and that's why she always disappeared into the thicket behind mother's house whenever the ground under her feet trembled in announcement of his coming. She could afford to take off, especially when his presence was not directly connected with her. But now she couldn't. Outside the darkness stared at her. And she knew just why he'd come. Though in her sixteen years of life she had never given him cause to complain, she knew nevertheless what a source of worry she was to him. He viewed her beauty as a burden on his shoulders, and she herself as the fated chick that would attract the demonic hawks into Gakoh family.

"Lemea! put your eyes into my eyes!" he snapped as soon as he set his eyes on her. His fury had mellowed somewhat but his voice was still sufficiently hard to jolt her backwards.

"Uncle," I interrupted in anguished sympathy.

"Is your name Lemea?" Uncle Abua shot back.

"Is my waist beaded?" I ventured jokingly. The trick worked somehow: Uncle Abua's tight lips relaxed into an ugly horizontal line. Whenever it came to me, the nephew he proudly called his son, affection dripped through every pore in his skin. He always said something about me reminded him so much of his own father. Was it the physical resemblance? Maybe.

"You know, my son," he would say in moments of affection, "You are tall in a handsome way. You are like the Creator's morning work. There are few like you who leave the divine workshop in the morning. My father Ewung Gakoh was one of them. And then you fish well. And the girls like you." He would accompany this last statement with long laughter.

All these things he said provided him daily nourishment for his interest in me. Of course he would himself have been the happier for possessing some of these strengths he recognized in me, especially my easy way with women. He knew that he could always impose himself on them, as he had done on his only wife, but there were times he missed the sublime reward of natural charm; times, too, when he wished his name, like mine, governed the lips of women in Nwemba. That he was not at the centre of little gossips in the village nipped from time to time at the edges of his manly pride. But he took his fortunes in good stride; indeed happily. His wife was enough of a blessing, what with his bizarre ways she had covered him like a mother hen would place an insouciant chick away from the hungry swoops of hawks. What was more, the gods had placed in his very hands a moral responsibility over Gakoh family in which he perceived a clear sign of their special favour. There was perhaps the explanation: he could not be scourge and cure. The gods wanted him to cure, not to breed decay. A feeling of pride surged up in him.

"Lemea has been with me since the chicks went to roost," I pressed on. "She returned just after mother left for your compound. In fact their two dusts mingled. She's been here since then helping me to mend my fishing net. Ma-Nina sent for her. She wanted her to talk to Nina. Ma-Nina complains that Nina is leading a life in which she does not see her own life-long example and each time she tries to talk Nina screams in her face that she is no longer a little girl to be dictated to by withered breasts."

"Lemea, put your eyes in my eyes!" Uncle bellowed, choking almost with anger. His conciliatory mood, hard-won by my tricks, had vanished. "Is what I'm hearing true?"

I looked painfully at the arms of my bamboo chair as they creaked under the angry man's conclusive clasp.

"Is it true that Nina has become dirt? What have you to do with a creature like that, eh? You say you went to advise her. Prrr! Tell me you went to be coached by her. I know that's what took you to that house. But let me tell you one thing. This family will not be smeared. You hear? This family will not be the dumping ground for any filth. Dinga of Meamba has approached me about you. I've already given him my word and it will be him. On your marriage day your mother and I will have to walk with an upright head with pride in our hearts. On that day your dead father must beat his chest with pride. If you have an ounce of Gakoh blood in you, think of that day."

One of those sporadic dry-season rainstorms was about. They came in sudden, violent downpours. When they came in the day they offered a pleasant spectacle of loose skirts flying over heads, and of excited children baring their beaming tummies to the big drops. This one came in the night, when sleep was sweetest to children and when age-bent elders relieved over palmwine the mythic exploits of their youth.

Uncle Abua had the good mind to defy the storm but somehow he allowed my protests to have the better of him.

"You are right," he said. "I can receive a falling plantain stem on my head and bring a great sorrow on the family."

Although he was no man to fear falling plantain stems, the sudden thought of dying and leaving Gakoh family without a shepherd made the showdown unnecessary. He sank back into his chair, its arms groaning to his angered grip.

"Before men I am invincible, but not before the gods. They may bring a plantain stem down on my head and carry me away with my work unfinished. Such is their ways. Unknowable beings. I will wait for all the falling plantain stems to reach earth."

He bent forward and caught his head in his two hands, his elbows planted on his knees. It was only now that Lemea stirred to life again. She listened and thought she heard Uncle breathing heavily. I dismissed her with a nod and she slipped out.

The rain ceased and the wind fell. Uncle Abua slapped his face with cold water from my earthen pot and offered his body to the night. I locked my door after him and crossed to mother's house to say goodnight.

The house was smoke-filled. A ritual. That was the way she liked her house. She said smoke was the best cure for rheumatism, *lumatisi*, as she called it. Lemea was already asleep, her face tear-stained and tired.

"What did your uncle do to her?" Mother queried, sitting up on her earthen bed. She stoked the fire with a long bamboo that lay permanently by her bed for that purpose, and gave life to an arresting mixture of embers and thick-particled smoke that quivered upwards to the neatly-worked bamboo ceiling.

"He was harsh to her, very harsh. You know his obsession with the honour of our family. He sees evil everywhere, in everything, in everybody. He thinks that the girls in the family, Lemea and his own daughter Minda especially, are nothing but the devil's palmwine bush."

"I don't know, my child. In my days…"

"Mother, don't return to your days. This thing is nothing to do with time but with a way of seeing things."

"You are a man, my son, and you know better. Has Olembe sent for his carving?"

"No. I promised to deliver it to him this evening but it's too late now. I'll go there first thing tomorrow morning. Good night mother."

"Good night, my son."

I did not look for my bed though my drooping eyes begged me to do so. Instead I felt my way to my stool and sat down. The thickening darkness lent an unusual sensation to my loneliness, so that I felt at the same time uplifted as if by some exhilarating force and bogged down as one would be by a heavy stone.

Figures began to form out of the night. Different shapes flashed past my eyes, some recognizable, others foreign. One figure in particular hovered around longer than the others. It was the shape of a tall muscular man with eyes powerful enough to move even the heaviest objects. It carried a red stone in its right hand and darkness oozed from its left hand to shroud the stone. I winked hard to drive it away. That particular shape was too familiar to find a place in the privacy of my late night loneliness.

The dance of figures ended and I recovered some of my thinking powers. Lemea's late homecoming, my rebuke of her – the scenes flocked into my head as I sat staring into the darkness, seeing nothing, only smelling the dank smell of bamboo-ash that filled the room. Lemea did not empty her heart to me. There's something she is hiding from me. Her face did not speak a frank language. I know Lemea. Her mouth said one thing, her face another. She has never hidden anything from me but this evening she did. When a girl starts hiding things from her brother it means there's a man in her life. Who could that man be? Why does my mind remain so blank? Or is it… no! the gods forbid!

As I felt my way into bed I heard Nwemba cocks sending their first greetings in the direction of Meamba. The answer came in fading tunes that left only a soft echo in the head.

No sleep. Only Lemea. Lemea…what kind of girl was this? See the confusion she was throwing about just when the family was thinking seriously about her marriage. Aunt Sabina would arrive any time from Tazim, half a day's trek from Nwemba, in the direction of Fetet. She had sent news already that she would be spending one week with us to prepare Lemea for marriage. Clan matron, she was the one in charge of marriage, both for the girls in the clan going to marry out of it and for girls from outside entering the clan.

So far she had not encountered any difficulty. But with Lemea one could never tell. She was the kind to ask: What is the urgency? One would not be surprised to have such a question from her. There were many other startling things she was quite capable of saying: This preparation can be done in due course, many moons later. Why should my aunt risk her life for a thing that can be done any time? And who even told them that I am ready for marriage? I do not like the way the family is forcing these things on me. I've said so to Uncle Abua and will repeat the same thing to Aunt Sabina on this visit. I will leave her just enough time to rest from the tiring and dangerous journey, then I will let her know that I am now big enough to handle some of these matters myself. Aunt Sabina will not like such a statement – Uncle Abua hadn't liked it either. In fact the day I said to him that I will not allow another person to choose a husband for me, that such a thing was my business, he rose to slap me but I was quick enough to jump out of the house before the flying hand caught me.

A girl who did things like that was also capable of confronting her aunt with some disturbing talk: preparation for marriage is a thing of the mind first, and then only a formality with the rest of the family. All the time people

95

want you to run because that is the custom. What if they want you to run just when your body is not ready for such a thing? She was quite capable of asking.

And talking about running, that's how the little girls used to run away each time Njitifuh came to disrupt their playing. For no reason. Only because he wanted to show them that he was he and could kill their happiness when he liked. She too used to run away with the other little girls, even as something inside her kept saying don't run. Stand. Stand there and see what he will do to you. He has hands. You too. Stand. And then one day she had stood and waited for him. When he saw that she was not running away he became confused and started fumbling. First he stopped whistling that his whistle, then he started looking for his steps like one with jiggers on all his ten toes. He was lucky that he didn't enter the tabala design where she was standing. She would have entered his legs and remained there until she felt him on the ground. Then she would have sat on him and hit him hard with her both hands and called the other girls to join her. He was lucky.

The other little girls had asked her whether she was not afraid that Njitifuh would beat her and maybe pierce one of her eyes or even both. She had only laughed and asked them whether she would be sleeping. What Aunt Sabina and the rest of the family wanted to put her through was not different from Njitifuh's intrusions into their play in Meamba.

She was even tempted not to open the door when her aunt finally arrived. That way she would go to her brother's house and meet him and then they would stay up all night thinking of what to do with this rebellious daughter. Uncle Abua would be only too happy to receive his little sister to whom he would narrate with a sweating face how his own niece had stood up to him in a way no child had ever done…you will not believe it, but what is this world coming to? Lemea, a child I carried in these my hands and washed her excrements. Today she says she's big enough to manage her own life…that I am exerting too much pressure on her. Since I did not break her jawbones on that day, I will never do it again. But I am waiting for her. She is either the daughter of Sama Gakoh or the bastard reject of a stray woman. What is this world coming to? Does she know what it means for me to say to Dinga and his family that they have wasted their time all these years? Sema's father died a shameful death. I hope that's not what she is preparing for me. I will not take it… With uncle and aunt in agreement, she was only a little bird in a cage. But she was capable of speaking her mind. This time at least. She would not let what had happened to her in Meamba repeat itself here. Maybe it was because she was still small then. She was big now and ready to have her way in certain things, especially those that concerned her. She hadn't been able to do this in Meamba. Her father had spoken for her, decided for her. Everyday she had sat by her mother in the little kitchen, sat there doing nothing, only waiting for her brother to return from school so that she opens the book with drawings and look at them with shining eyes. Her father had refused to see the hunger in her eyes. She would not allow herself to be forced one way again, against her wish.

How would she shield off her aunt's long talk on marriage? The woman would insist on inspecting her, on touching her in all kinds of intimate places to make sure she was still good for marriage. She remembered Sema, how her own aunt had driven her hand into her and said she was not fit for marriage, that any marriage that involved her would bring only shame to their family. She remembered how Sema had tied a cloth round her neck on the day she was to marry, and had been found hanging from the ceiling of her father's barn. No one was going to push her to such despair. She wouldn't allow her aunt to violate her intimacy. She wouldn't let her do it.

Not that she had anything to hide, or to fear.

She and Masutu had sat around a few times; it is true. That was something she liked to do with him. Sit around and at times allow him to touch her. Of all the young men circling around her, it was his voice she heard each time she closed her eyes and asked her heart to speak, as she often did on returning from a dance at which style and strength had competed for her notice. Tankeh Winjala danced well. On a fine day there was no dancer to equal him in the way his body met the calling of the rhythms. The way he closed ekwang celema had no equal in any of the villages around. A few times she had closed her eyes and caught his voice gnawing within her heart-walls. Once even, she had come close to saying yes to his invitation. Only fear of Uncle Abua had driven the temptation back. But now that the fear was dying away, she did not know how she would behave if a similar situation came up. She was not very sure what she would do.

As for Masutu, she didn't need to listen too hard to hear his voice inside her. It seemed to be a natural part of her. It was so familiar, so warm. If he held her hand she would follow, wherever he took her. There was no other man in Nwemba with such powers over her; no man who could enter her body and take control with no threat of resistance. She even hated the way her body belonged to him; but try as she might, she could not send away the surrender, or even reduce it.

She still remembered the last brush with disaster, when the luung dance had lasted late into the night and everyone had retired except a few diehards. Taiti had seized hold of the instrument and caught it between his legs. Then he had plucked its fingers the way only he alone could. She'd sat at a corner and watched Masutu move his body and had felt a sudden rush of passion seize her, ending in twitching sensations in her inner thighs. After the dance he'd wanted to touch her, even to hold her, and she'd struggled and fought, not against him but against herself, until she'd succeeded in breaking away and running — flying — to their house.

The marriage plans bringing Aunt Sabina in from Tazim were one of those vexations she could have done without. The family elders talked only about Dinga. It was Dinga here, Dinga there. Dinga had done this. Dinga had done that. Dinga's family. Palmwine. Bundles of kolanut. And she? Who had cared? Who had asked how she thought of that Dinga, or felt about him? Not even once had she sat close enough to the man to catch the smell of his body. So how did they think she would allow herself into life with a man even whose bodily smell she did not know?

She had tried to talk to them about Masutu but everybody had thrown her and her Masutu out. Only her brother understood her. But when it came to who she married, his opinion, like her own, did not count for much. The whole thing looked and sounded so funny to her. She was waiting to see how Aunt Sabina and Uncle Abua would bundle her into Dinga's house and keep her there through the rest of her life. She was just waiting to see. One thing she knew was that Nwemba was not Meamba.

She remembered the little conversation she'd had with mother in Meamba the day father talked about the first time he washed the things the white woman wore closest to her body. To the question what did a girl do if the parents she was waiting for did not come and only wrong parents came to see your father, she'd said you put your face in your palms and cried; and that as a girl you had no say in the decision taken in your father's house. You went where that decision sent you. So they wanted her to sit in her mother's house now and hear Dinga's parents talking and laughing in her father's house and drinking palmwine with Uncle Abua..

A knock interrupted her thoughts. She rose from her stool with a start and rushed to the door. But there was nobody there. And yet she was certain she had heard a knock. Night had fallen completely, so that unless a figure outside stood in the direct rays of the week fire in the house, it would not be seen. She stood at the door and peered outside and seeing nothing, closed the door and turned back. But as she was about to sit down, the knock came again. She grew apprehensive, even frightened. When she opened the door again there was still nobody, but this time a calabash was standing there. It did not contain palmwine but a rich harvest of rare, stubby caterpillars, the kind that only the richest raffia bushes could produce. Whoever put that calabash there must be someone who knew her and her taste.

Something said she should leave the calabash there at the door until her mother returned and either brought it into the house or threw it away if she so chose; that she could not collect a thing put in front of their door at night by invisible hands. But this thought did not stay for long in her head. Ever since she saw the stubby white things milling about in the calabash, her own body seemed to have caught the same fever. She was now alive, alert, eager. If anyone asked her now, just now, whether she was ready to marry she would say yes. It did not matter who asked her the question. Even Dinga, but preferably Masutu. She would say yes without looking back.

Those caterpillars seemed to have done something to her body. They had thrust her in the mood for marriage, freed her mind to the happiness of living under a man's roof and giving him children. Those caterpillars were like children – neat and well-fed, innocent in their joy. They were just a bit too many for the number of children she would like to deliver, but they looked to her the way she would like her children to be.

This was a tender moment. If Aunt Sabina dropped in just now she would get anything she wanted out of her. She was ready to say yes to any question her aunt put to her, ready to follow her to Uncle Abua's house and take any cup in her hands that was proposed to her.

It was an interesting thought to her that good things too could travel at night and find their rightful destinations.

Without any further thought, she stepped outside and brought in the calabash. Its content made pleasant sounds – pleasant little sounds, like meat sizzling in palmoil. She emptied the caterpillars to the floor and watched them wriggling with freshness – swollen beautiful things. She would have loved to keep them alive and watch them each time she wanted to feel happy. But she could not because they could not live long out of the comfort of the palm-bush.

She would roast some and treat her aunt to them, or her mother; and why not both of them? She would sizzle some in palmoil to go with steaming foo-foo, so that any of the old women who came in would have something delicious and warm to eat. She did not know where the gift was from and really did not bother that much. To anyone who questioned her about it she would say just that, and then would add that only a well-meaning person could make such a gift to her. Now that she thought of it, she would lay some in the barn to dry and then take them over to Uncle Abua. She knew he liked caterpillars, especially the thick type. He would receive them with a broad smile and then thank her.

The more she thought of the many things she could do with the caterpillars the more exciting the whole gift idea appeared to her. Who could have done such a thing? Until now, she would have sworn anything that Nwemba did not hold one soul that knew her inner thoughts and likings. Now she was baffled, even a little tickled.

When she was born her mother's breastmilk refused to flow. For many weeks she lived on caterpillars, without which she would have died. They fed her the white caterpillar juice that was just like breastmilk. That was the story her mother told her when she was old enough to appreciate the saving role of raffia palm caterpillars in her life. Now, many years afterwards, someone had linked her up with her childhood memories through a rich calabash delivered in all anonymous friendliness.

Chapter Nine

She wasn't with me. She wasn't here in any case. Not here. Not here... The words darted and kicked about in my head, knocked and whistled like sizzling meatballs in steaming oil. What a fool I'd been to stir the topic. Now I knew what I had feared to know. The shred of hope on which I had hung had snapped and I was tumbling, tumbling. How far down would I fall? What did the revelations hold for me? Now I knew that Lemea hadn't spent the evening with Olembe. I must seek out the truth. I must. Her reputation was my business. I was not going to have another man work my farm for me as if I had been stricken with leprosy. I was not a leper. My fingers, all ten of them, were in full health. Lemea was my farm, my plot of land. Recent happenings had shown me that it was growing into wild forest with monsters waiting in the shade. I was going to reclaim it, work it clean, chase away the monsters, destroy the reptiles, kill all the bad beasts. My father's dying words...I could hear them still in my ears... my daughter... He hadn't finished. Death had sealed his lips, leaving me with a half-finished whisper.

As if winged to the place by those half-finished words now come alive, I found myself chewing roast maize in Ma-Nina's house. I'd meant on leaving Olembe to go to my palm-bush and carry home the evening's harvest of palmwine. But here I was in Ma-Nina's house on a three-legged stool, with my back against a heap of freshly-harvested maize.

Nina handed me the roast maize at a steady rhythm. Questions followed the roasting and the eating, questions thrown in a way that did not show any worry. If Nina knew the fire burning inside me she would not tell me everything she knew, especially the bad ones.

Yes, she spent the whole afternoon and the better part of the evening here with me. No, my mother was not in all through. She cooked, then collected her hoe and went behind the house to finish her cocoyam beds. What we talked about? Why do you want to know what we did and what we talked about? You want to know everything, just for the pleasure of it. Call me stubborn again. You cannot dig into our secrets like that.

Another roast maize was handed to me which I waved back protesting: "You haven't had any yourself."

"A mother eats through her child," she said, then clapped the coal dust off her hands and placed both hands on the upper part of her half-stretched legs, her face lit with a dignity at odds with her age. There was something really maternal about her now that had not been there before that deep reflection on the joys of motherhood.

"This child part again," I protested somewhat humorously. "Who is your child here anyway?"

"What are you? Or are you saying you've grown so big you are not my child any more? Who else feeds you apart from me? I know one or two names…they do not bother me…only let me tell you… a child has only one mother. I delivered you…you will never grow too big to be my child."

"I thank you for it. But will you now say I should not grow up and walk on my own feet? One can never talk strong talk with you. Ahah!"

Strong talk. She turned at this and faced me.

"I knew something drove you out of your house today."

"Nina, Lemea came home late last night."

"If it is that one you will run here. When did I last see you?"

"You will see me any time you like. But now I need help. There are ants in our house."

"Let them bite those your feet well well."

"Nina...Lemea. It was not only that she came home late. She was nervous and agitated in a way I'm not used to seeing her."

"Not bleeding and her clothes torn and her body in mud."

"No."

"She came home safely, only agitated."

"Safely, I don't know."

"Where is she now?"

"Why? At home."

"You should have told me all this from the beginning instead of sitting there and eating all my maize and pretending that you just came to visit me."

"Visit is in this too, Nina."

"I've not said no. But it's more because of Lemea that you came."

"Nina, take this stone out of my throat."

"My child, nothing is wrong. Only that you men cannot understand. Lemea was lively yesterday as usual. Only, she started to hold her belly and hold it more and more tight. You men cannot understand this kind of thing. You do not know that pains can enter a girl's stomach in the middle of laughter."

The grating sound of a hoe being cleaned outside announced Ma-Nina's return from the farm. I jumped to my feet and slipped out through the back door.

My steps devoured the path. They were quick and sturdy, like the homebound strides of a rewarded hunter. Victory swelled and broke in me, and flooded my whole body with surging waves of success.

And why not? Nina had chased away all my fears with her answers and the other things she said, especially that one about a pain entering a girl's stomach in the middle of laughter and irritating her nerves, and that other one about men not knowing or understanding that this pain could damage even the toughest of nerves. Such was the world of women – a closed, mysterious little world in which men wandered like lost goats, not knowing how it worked, not understanding its details.

My eyes searched the path as if to seek answers to the many questions about the ways of women. Suddenly, to my left, close by, rose the sudden moan of palmtrees and the slash of a machete bleeding them of their white blood. A shiver drove through me, straight through, killing my joy. The path darkened. A strange sensation descended on me. I felt the presence of an aggressive energy, the furious charge of a dark force. My face heated as if spanked by fire. My palms moistened so much that I had to rub them against my bare arms which were also running with sweat.

In a strange yet still accurate manner the scene of my first brush with death came to my mind... the sun's shimmering glow, the sweat on my body, the fluffy caress of pollen rising from the grass that fell to the swing of my machete...my father Sama Gakoh at the far end of the farm resting under a giant plumtree.

The noise of my labour had reached him in soft waves and soon he had fallen asleep, knees in an upturned V, head resting against the trunk, hands folded on his bare stomach. I remembered the falling grass, then... a half-coiled mamba. I closed my eyes, but all I heard was a dying hiss.

"Lemea! Lemea!" I called from the crest of the little hill overlooking our compound. The night had set in already firmly but the pale overhead moon still threw some light about. The moon lingered with stubbornness, as if sent by nature to see me home safely before retiring. I called out again as no answer rewarded my first attempt. I stood steadfast on the crest, looking out in the direction of our compound, expecting Lemea to run out of mother's house and fall in my embrace. It didn't occur to me one moment that I had ruined the day's programme with my many errands across the village, that by spending long hours at Olembe's and later with Nina I had left my share of the day's work undone. I didn't see either that I had given mother this day as the last on which to build the yam-barn she'd asked me to build many weeks back. All I wanted, the only strong wish in me on that crest was that Lemea should leave everything she was doing and fly to me so that I could feel the warmth of her integrity.

For what was barn-building compared with the dangers threatening our family? I could build the barn any time, right now, tomorrow, many days later. But there were other higher worries, other bigger barns. And what had happened to my sister, or hadn't happened – I was still not so sure – was one of such worries. Like a cherished egg crushed by a bad leg, a lost good name could not be brought back; not by any amount of weeping. Lemea was an egg and no matter was more important, more urgent than placing her beyond harm.

One thing I knew as I stood on that crest washed by the pale moonlight, and that one thing was that I had put Lemea beyond the reach of all the cancerous whims in Nwemba. She was my lost pearl regained. I had won her back through a stubborn fight both with myself and with the forces of evil. A hard fight with myself first, for I had had to silence in me the guilt of destroying in other homes what I sought so eagerly to preserve in my own.

Homes like Ta-Nina's. I had done some bad things with Nina, bad things which, if done to my own sister, would have destroyed my pride for always. Nina and I had locked bodies in the most unclean manner in all kinds of places and at all kinds of times. I had waited for her right behind her mother's house and she had come. I had whistled to her from the left bank of Mantum and she had swum across, reaching me in wet clothes and a wet body which lit a blazing fire in my flesh. I had devoured the wetness, feeling her tender fingers as they roamed the supporting grass in search of a place for her thumping breasts.

I'd had to wage a big fight with myself, to convince my conscience that Lemea was different from Nina and had to be treated specially. That is why I didn't want to confront Ma –Nina on her return from the farm. I didn't want to see myself in her eyes, to see in those eyes the untold accusations of an abused mother. And so I sneaked out like a thief surprised in the moments prior to looting.

I was both disease and cure, both thief and anti-thief, builder and destroyer, all in one breath. Lemea was to be preserved and protected, Nina to be used according to the whims of my animal instincts. With Nina I was a man, alive only to the age-old drive of animal passion; with Lemea I was a brother, protective, jealous to obsession; a brother who subsumed all his life in the respect of a father's dying half whisper. This was the brother calling out from the crest of the hill, calling out into an increasingly impatient visibility.

The stamp, stamp of approaching footsteps beset my ears. The steps were ugly. A man visited with such steps could not win a dance contest in Nwemba, let alone Fetet. He would be mad to enter one in the first place. He could not walk past and leave admiration behind him either.

The moon had disappeared, giving way to a thick black night. I darted off the path. It wasn't like me to run away from approaching footsteps, but an inner voice ordered me this time to the act. I didn't question the good sense in what I was doing. I just did it. Better quarrel with this inner voice in safety than stand planted on that path and meet trouble. I had barely left the path when the approaching footsteps drew abreast of me. I saw their owner in the black night. On his muscular shoulders rode two pots of fresh palmwine.

I did not come out of hiding immediately. I remained there for some time, feeling the prickle of ferns on my leg-sides, wondering why Lemea hadn't answered my call, thanking the inner voice for steering me away from potential danger, admiring my sense of discipline at not having questioned that inner voice. I remained in the bush thinking of the present to make to Lemea now that I knew – or almost – that she was as she'd always been. When I finally came out of my hiding I made straight for mother's house and ordered Lemea over to my house, with little heed to mother's queries about my long absence and late homecoming.

Lemea followed me. Her steps were silent, almost inaudible. Her face was pale. It didn't give the impression of sadness; it just looked pale. There was something intriguing about the whole face, something which urged one to scratch beneath the skin to discover in the veins the root of the paleness. And yet on looking at her closely one felt that it would be wrong to violate the secrecy of her worries. The paleness was not static. It was changing, so that now she appeared calm, even distant, now tired, dying for rest, yet itching for activity.

I took a long, stern look at her. I sized up her feelings, trying to grasp what lay in her head. My imaginative powers were on the charge. They surged forward, broke against the still paleness on her face, returned to base, gathered strength, surged out again, and again they foundered on the impassive look on her face.

I locked the charging forces up and resorted to dialogue. I had called her to talk and talk I would.

"My own stool... sit on it." My voice was magnified by the absence of other noises. "You have changed a lot since yesterday evening. You talk little, you laugh little. Anything to do with me?" I did not wait for an answer but continued, as if in a monologue. "I didn't like the time you returned home and that's why I spent the whole of this day running after the truth."

She shifted imperceptibly on her stool.

"A feeling entered my head yesterday night that evil had seized you. But now I can say those bad thoughts were bad thoughts only. It is better to have fears turned to nothing than to be overtaken by evil."

She did not answer but carried her head as if it was a baby. I rose and took her by the arm and accompanied her to mother's house before returning to lock myself up in my own house.

The lingering perplexity of the evening now built into a threatening force that I could no longer ignore. Her silence had given me assurance. But the silence had vanished, so that now I was tormented by doubt, eaten by uncertainty.

I forced myself to bed but could not force myself to sleep. My eyes danced in my head, rolling here and there for what to cure my tortured mind with. They danced and danced, rolled and darted until they hit the heap of carved objects at the left corner; figurines and busts, masks, bas-relief, drums and utensils.

One of the figurines was that of the white man. My eyes settled on that one and soon, inside deep sleep, it jumped alive. In the place of the figurine now stood the white man talking – talking to the people of Meamba muted, like flock before a shepherd. Work, work and work. Think. Heads. Or disappear. Or be crushed. Crushed already…down… pit will swallow you. Villager puts up hand… thinking different from theirs? You have not been thinking… not of the right things…the road…I had to come…you have not been thinking… the small hospital…I had to come…you think… how many women…the pregnant ones…many die…you think… calabashes of wine…villagers laugh… fall over one another in laughter…white man carries hands to ears… Stop! Cry! Craiiii….!

The white man's shout was long and strong. I jumped out of sleep and only saw the carved objects staring at me.

This was the first time, since I started working with wood, that my products shook me like this. My mind went back to Okran. It was because of him that I decided to become a carver. One book we were taught in the white man's big school in Ediki-Mbeng was called *Fragments*, and it was written by a man called Ayi Kwei Armah. Okran was a man in this book. He was an artist and a teacher. All the children he taught left him and did other things in life. Some went into medicine, some into engineering, others even into law. None of them followed his example. Yet he was such a sound man. So when I saw the way he was complaining I decided that I would be the follower he never had. He was also very good at advising people. He told the dreamy one Baako who returned from the white man's country that if he wanted to do any real work in that their country he must work alone. When Baako asked to know what he meant, the artist said nobody in that their country was interested in being serious.

I put what Okran said to Baako, and the white man's shouting voice in my sleep side by side and saw that they were like twin brothers. Okran to me was not different from the white man. He saw what was wrong, where the dirt was. He said people were not interested in being serious. That was just another way of saying they only slept, like dogs in the sun. And the white man saw it too that way. And came to me in my sleep and entered Okran's wood.

Chapter Ten

Aunt Sabina had arrived from Tazim the following day and chosen to live with Uncle Abua instead. Good news for Lemea; at least she would not be under the woman's nose for tormenting instructions on marriage. Why did she even bother about where her aunt lived? For all she cared, the woman could live with them and pester her every single day on who to marry and how to behave in her marriage. She had prepared a set attitude for all situations. She ran a sample encounter with her aunt over in her mind and laughed in satisfaction at the way she kept the woman at bay; no easy exercise if one thought of Aunt Sabina's tactics, all made of sweet language and tempting references to her own experience. Her power of conviction had sent many girls of the family to marriages they had not sued for; and it was known in a wide circle that whenever she set to work, the marriage was as good as sealed.

Lemea knew what to expect now that her aunt had come. She knew that the woman would rest for just one day, if at all, then she would send for her. She always liked to talk to the family girls in the presence of Uncle Abua, who lent her the support of manliness and scolding if it came to that.

She would go if her aunt sent for her, but would remain defiant. Not rude. Only steadfastly defiant – no I am not going to marry Dinga. My daughter! Auntie, I do not know the man you are talking about. I did not know my own man before I entered his house. You are you and I am me. Just wait. What am I hearing? Lemea, put your eyes in my eyes.

She would. She would look her uncle straight in the eyes and keep her eyes there. She has. Can you see? No more fear. No more respect. Never mind. You can look at me for as long as you like, but you will marry Dinga. That's the way it is done in this family. Uncle, I do not know the man you are talking about. I do not know the man, I do not know the man. How do you know a man? And what do you mean by *knowing* a man? There's only one way of knowing a man and it is by marrying him. Uncle, I cannot marry a man I do not know. Leave the matter to me…you will, unless you are not my daughter.

Uncle Abua would storm out in anger cursing to himself. Aunt Sabina would draw her seat closer and place her heavy right arm on her shoulder – My daughter, marriage is a thing of pride for the family. Auntie, marriage should be a thing of pride for those who marry first. My daughter, bad thoughts. These things you say are things to put sadness in the family. Auntie, it is instead what you say that will put sadness in the hearts of those who marry. Which god shall I call for help? Laikum? Or Belahmandji? None of the gods, Auntie. Only give happiness to those who marry. And the family? Those who marry: that's the family.

She did not know how her aunt would take this, but that was the attitude she would put on all through. She was ready for the insults and threats, but she was not going to shed any of her determination.

When she stirred out of the rehearsal she caught the sound of drums from Chief Ndelu's palace. A rhythm had sorted itself out of the initial mix so that there was now a steady rise and fall of the male drum, a variation of the powerful and the sublime in the rhythmic appeal. The hamlet of Nwemba was alive. The stars above, too, were warming up for the dance.

The sounds that came could only be the work of Benti Edinge. His fingers produced rhythms on drums with rare virtuosity; his voice caressed tunes in a manner that brought tears of admiration to the eyes of many women. When he took to the floor everyone else became a muted spectator of his ordained performance.

114

I knew Benti Edinge's voice well for having listened to it many times before. The voice I was hearing now was unmistakably Edinge's. "Ekpan celema e e e ekpan celema!" This was the magic tune with which he always prefaced a dance session. It was a tune for men, a song that stretched the fibres of manliness to snapping point. I jumped to my feet, rent the air with two curt slashes and made for mother's house. My crossing of the compound was a rehearsal stint that I used to check out my responses.

My spirits plunged as I met Lemea staring emptily into the weak bamboo flames in the fireplace. I went and sat by her.

"I thought you would be ready by now. You hear that? Those drums are beating for us. They invite the strong limbs of Nwemba, the fine bodies of Nwemba to come and fill Chief Ndelu's hall with sweat and dust. Ready yourself for it."

"I will try on my bangles," she said, rather dutifully.

"It is running late. Edinge intoned Ekpan celema already. Even now I can hear the excitement."

"In that case, you go and let me know tomorrow how it went."

I said with mild irritation: "What can I do to win your company to the dance this evening? Just let me know and I will do it."

"I don't know. I want to take my mind away from the dance. Help me. Tell me something different… a nice little story…anything that does not remind me of the dance…our village, for example. Tell me where we came from and how we got here."

"That's a long story."

"Tell me all the same."

Lemea moved from the stool by the fireplace to the bamboo bed and lay on her side. Her head was propped up by her left hand, the elbow of which was planted on a supporting mound. Her both legs were drawn up so that her knees provided a good resting place for her half-stretched right arm. Her loincloth, dyed in plantain-leaf designs, covered her body from knee to armpit and the other bare parts reflected softly in the unattended flickers.

I grew suddenly solemn and switched my mind to the mythic exploits of Nwembwana.

"We are a village of farmers and fishermen," I intoned, very much in the manner of Chief Ndelu's teller, "but we haven't always lived here. We were brought here many seasons ago by Nwembwana, the patriarch of our village. The story goes that back in the ancestral land of Bengeta, many, many moon's trek from here, an epic fight opposed him to his half-brother Ilembea. They fought for many days, matching strength with strength, for both of them were equal in battle. The elders were aggrieved by the sight of such fierce rivalry. They put their heads together and decided that one of the rivals seek a new home beyond the hills. Strangely enough, the decision fell on Nwembwana, not Ilembea, the large-mouthed one who provoked the fight.

"Ilembea would have been the one to suffer exile for having started the trouble, but he had been so badly damaged in the fight that there was not much of him left to be exiled. And so the sanction had fallen on Nwembwana since one person had to go for peace to return to Bengeta.

"Nwembwana took along with him his young wife Seala, two moons heavy with child."

The flicker in the fireplace had died out completely so that a thorough darkness now enveloped us. I was even unaware of the death of the flames, so wrapped was I in my story. Nor did I notice that Lemea had long since lowered her head onto the mound and was now battling with strange presences.

"Nwembwana did not depart alone from Bengeta. Tindu Winjala went with him, carrying along his three wives and eighteen children. Tandag, the one-legged trapper, Forchap Alembeng, keeper of Bengeta's ritual fishing net, these two also threw in their lot with the exiled Nwembwana.

"The party journeyed for many moons, following the course of Mantum which rose from the rocky escarpment just above Bengeta and provided a natural boundary with the Fetets, a new settler group attracted to the area by news of Bengeta's masquerade prodigies. Nwembwana led the way, keeping closely to the course of Mantum, until they reached Meamba. Chief Walang, the tall, ripe-palmfruit-coloured Chief of Meamba commended all round for his smooth ways, welcomed Nwembwana and his people to his palace and asked to be told the circumstances of their exile. The homeless ones were impressed with the young chief's reaction to the story. He blamed Nwembwana, even chided him, for having allowed himself to be dragged into a meaningless fight. Real force, he cautioned, did not lie in the careless use of brute energy but rather in the calm ability to withstand provocation.

"For three moons Chief Walang kept and feasted the exiled ones.

"The journey had weakened Seala very much. She had entered Meamba leaning wearily on Alembeng's shoulder. More than three times on the long journey they had had to stop and give her time to catch some extra sleep and reassemble herself. Soon upon their arrival in Meamba she had presented both the arriving ones and the host Chief with a boy. Nwembwana had immediately named his son Walangji, the child of the good one, in permanent memory of Walang's goodness to them.

"The three moons spent in Chief Walang's court had brought new strength into Seala's limbs so that by the fourth moon they were set to resume the trek. As they departed the Chief put his finger in the air and advised that they follow the direction of the wind until they came to a hillock dotted with barren pear trees. Upon reaching that place they were to collect water from the flowing river, all of them, and pour it on the barren trees and found their settlement around the hillock.

"You see where Tankeh Winjala's house stands? It was in that same place that Nwembwana performed the ritual act of possession of Nwemba. That is the birthplace of the village, the womb in which mother earth carried the dreams of an exiled people and patiently, lovingly, nursed them into the reality that Nwemba has become today. Until Chief Ndelu gave the place to Tankeh Winjala, it was a sacred ground, anointed by the spoken and silent wishes of the people of this village."

No sound came to acknowledge the end of my narrative. It was only now that I was struck by the darkness and the silence, broken only lightly by Lemea's cadenced breathing.

Just as I reached into the hearth to stir the sleeping flames awake, a tortured shriek jolted me. I stayed my advancing hand and listened. Groans followed the shriek, then some mumbling protestations. I was afraid of what would come next. I reached for the bed in the darkness and shook Lemea by the leg. As she stirred I lit the fire again. She was sweating slightly, and trembling as well.

"How much of the story did you hear?" I asked, almost needlessly.

"Not much. Sleep carried me away. I'm not sure I want to attend the dance. Please Banda, can you go alone? Olembe and Yeisi will certainly be there. You will not lack company."

"The dance without you will be meaningless. I want to see you happy, Lemea. You haven't been yourself since yesterday evening. Your face has lost its radiance. I just hope you are still only hurting from Uncle Abua's sternness."

"Yes, yes," she spurted absentmindedly, and fell silent again as if struck by instant dumbness. I observed her closely for clues to the deepening enigma. Whereas the previous day I had returned from Ma-Nina's house convinced that I had touched the heart of the matter, the more I watched my sister now the more my confusion deepened. Was there a malevolent design I could not perceive? Had Lemea broken any of the family moral rules and was now toiling under the weight of guilt? How could her face in just one day change into a dry bit of wood? Had she become home to the many devils amok in the hills of Nwemba? Why only her? Could they not have chosen a dwelling place in another body? I wished and prayed that my thoughts would remain thoughts only; that they would not transform into some ugly reality.

Since Lemea's yes, yes, she had regained the reposeful aspect of a baby stirring from sleep on its mother's breast. Her face had recovered some of its habitual smoothness so that now as I roamed my anxious eyes over her it seemed to me that I was rediscovering the sister I used to know, not a strange, possessed creature with the body and voice of my sister.

"Lemea, my sister, we will attend the dance," I exhorted, my voice suppressing the rhythms from Chief Ndelu's hall. Lemea did not answer. She only nodded, as if to say so be it. I seized on the opening. "You hear the drums? They are not beating. They are calling. They have looked inside the hall and not seen their favourite dancers. They have looked inside and not seen you. Go wear your beads. Oil your breasts and smoothen your ankles with calmwood. Mark your cheeks and dot your forehead. Let the bangles spread from your wrists to your elbows and the beads climb from your ankles to your knees. Come out like the lone star in the evening sky."

The praise exhortations did the trick. Like clotted palmoil in the morning sun, Lemea's whole body melted into a blanket of jelly-like tissue trembling for action. She leapt out and raced to my house and back, her mind all the while transforming her body into the lone star of the evening sky.

Chapter Eleven

Tankeh Winjala's house stood at some distance away from the village centre, so that if Nwemba was a living organism that house would not be anywhere near its heart but somewhere at the extremities from where, like bunions, it would jot out.

The distance of that house from the heartthrob of Nwemba was made bigger still by the smug compactness of the village itself which lay nestled together, like chicks burrowing into their mother's wings. The roofs pieced into a blanket sheath with only tiny openings between them; in certain places they were so close that they blended uninterruptedly into each other, eave to eave, whole house to whole house.

The track separating it from the heart of the village was not long; not the kind of distance that required getting up in the young hours of the morning to cover. In fact the house could be seen from any part of the village even if from certain points, like from Chief Ndelu's palace, watching it filled one with a sizzling sensation of distance. Only, there was no other house so remote as this one, no other house draped in such an eerie mantle of aloofness.

But for all its being eccentric, Tankeh Winjala's house still was, like a nail on a toe, part of Nwemba. Nwemba felt its distant presence, lived it. It lay at the same time outside the village and within it. Its twin aura of being and not being shrouded it in a uniqueness that was both attractive and intriguing. Nwembans felt both fascination and repulsion. They could not talk about Tankeh Winjala's house without a puzzling sensation of familiarity.

121

Not many people had been inside the house. Tankeh lived alone, as if in self-imposed solitary confinement. No wife. No children. One cock, too old to be eaten. No hens. A weird force enveloped his existence, and his house. Apart from the sturdy neatness of their bamboo panelling, the external aspects of his house would have passed it off for just any ordinary house in the village. The enigma of the inside did not seethe through.

The house stood on a mound, on that same rise where the patriarch Nwembwana had driven his spear into the crackled ground in a double act of victory and possession. That place had remained a sacred ground for many seasons, acting as shrine and libation place. Maybe on account of its forbidding aspect, it had gone down well as a dwelling place for the gods. The few withered pear trees and scanty panting grass about provided a natural setting for a pantheon.

But out of boredom of the gods or man's innate urge for change, the functions of the parched mound had been moved to the lush marshy shores of Mantum, somewhere just before the river swerved into a fall. Nwemba now poured libation amid a permanent, sun-creased cloud of surging drops from the crashing waters of the Mantum.

Tankeh Winjala had taken possession of the abandoned sacred place almost immediately afterwards. Not a defiant act. No. The place had come to him as a reward for halting Nwemba's eight-season-old shame in wrestling bouts with Tazim. Season after season, eight seasons long, Nwemba had returned from combat with Tazim cowed by defeat, numbed by shame. Old mothers had gone about naked. Many times shrivelled breasts had been bared in agony to heedless gods. An old woman's sorrow is a thing to dread. But the ancestors had not hearkened. No heed. Nwemba was forlorn. Then Tankeh Winjala had come, grown into manhood, not many moons after his father Winjala the Crude brought him back from Meamba at the abrupt end of his service to the white man. He hadn't only ended the run of shameful defeats; he had silenced many Tazim wrestlers with the violent arrogance of a wounded fighter. In the end Tazim had sued, and Chief Ndelu had used the truce to settle Tankeh Winjala on the site once the dwelling place of the gods.

Wrestling was good sport among the youth of Meamba; at least in the days when Winjala the Crude worked there as gardener to Pete Harrington. Everyday, as he left for the white man's house, he would call his son to his side and give the cautions of a father who knew where he was going: "That place where the white man has gathered children and ordered them to sing in his language is not for you. That their song will not help you when we return. It will not tap palmwine for you or hunt the cutting-grass. Your chance is in the wrestling field. You must be a man. You must not grow into a woman like Sama Gakoh's son who spends his day singing in the white man's tongue."

Repeated with fatherly conviction, these words had come to frame a son's window on the world as an opening down which wrestling stood as the only way to achievement. Tankeh attended wrestling sessions not only to fight but to defeat. Wrestling prepared him for hunting and tapping; wrestling drove the white man's songs away.

From his house Tankeh could catch the faint sounds of the male drums rippling in from the palace. Outside the crackling fire there were no other noises in his house to deform the drumbeats. They sailed into his ears with the same rhythmic purity with which they left the palace, only slightly weakened by the distance. They made good music to listen to. The male drums especially spoke to the man in him and his chest muscles trembled in response. The invitation was powerful, irresistible. He would be there.

Dance was his own thing. Even if music took second place to tapping, he nevertheless placed it among the things he liked doing best. He did not dance to win awards. He danced for the personal enrichment that music brought to his life. It made him light. It put a certain kind of sensation in him that he found hard to express. He just felt the feeling. The encounter of sweat and dust on his quivering shoulders always caused a special tremor to climb into his head; a kind of tremor that nothing, except maybe sleeping with a woman for the first time, would give.

Dancing and sleeping with a woman were twin delights. The intensity, the fulfilment, the ecstasy, the way the body tore itself apart into pounding sites of sensual delight, the heave, and the silence that sanctioned the act, no other happening commanded the body with greater power. It was in sleeping with a woman that man fulfilled himself. The woman's body was all Nwemba put together. Life and death were in it; happiness and doom too. Anything you did not find in a woman's body you would not find anywhere else, except in dance.

And it was there that his father's wisdom revealed itself again to him. This music shaking his body to life was nothing else but his father's words speaking to him. That music was language; language carrying the breath breathed by those who saw behind and in front. And his father was now one of them. He could see behind to when they were in Meamba; when he refused to call the grass the white man's grass; when he carried home a big monkey just like any one he would hunt in the adjoining forests of Nwemba. He could see in front, see clearly into the fishing contest to come and how it would be fought. Was he not telling his son that this dance was a dance of celebration?

Tankeh jumped to his feet and broke into dance.

Chapter Twelve

The hall was taut, not least because of the royal presence. Chief Ndelu sat enthroned on his teak stool, the scooped seat of which was borne by three half-raised tigers whose hind paws gripped the earth with totemic power. Two bare-chested court attendants stood watch over the chief at whose feet sat two princesses, one by each foot, this one bearing a bowl of palmwine, the other a tray of cola nuts. Ndelu chewed and sipped, and his face swept the man-filled hall with the serene airs of a happy ruler.

The first male drums went. They were manned by Sanu Edinge, Benti Edinge's senior man. Sanu knew his way with drums. He had beaten them to chiefs, newly married young men and their wives, corpses; he had drummed hearts to tears and minds to blowing point; he was even known to have made a two-day-old corpse twitch in admiration.

Sanu Edinge worked the male drums. As his hands descended on the skins, his head bent and twirled, and his shoulders heaved to the effort. Feet shuffled in excited approval, sending up thin sheets of dust.

Benti Edinge burst into the hall chanting to the accompaniment of rattles. The muscles on his stooping body shook, thrusting him forward in the direction of Chief Ndelu. As he approached the Chief rose to ululations and waving of whisks. Benti Edinge knelt before the Chief, backing him, and felt the royal hand pat its blessings on both his shoulder blades. The singer sprang forward, circled round the hall and stopped in front of the male drums and the xylophones. A brief silence punctuated the moment, then rattles rent the air again and the drums and the xylophones fell in.

The hall was now a sight of swaying feet lost in the powdery caress of brown dust.

A first spate of dancers bounded forward and shot their colourful whisks into the dust-filled air. The whisks surged and fell, surged and fell with unified purpose.

It was now that Tankeh Winjala entered the hall. Not many saw him enter, but it was not long before his presence filled the hall. First the damask cloth across his shoulder was unique in design and voluminous enough to attract attention from any point in the hall. As for his own whisk, it was those of four people tied together, and its presence in the air was always a celebration of magnificence. Even I felt captivated, seized by a certain power I could not fight off. I had never felt this way before, even though I had heard many other people in Nwemba confess to having come under such a spell.

The floor started to empty, and soon only the dust was left dancing.

Tankeh Winjala did not jump to action. He stood erect at the far end of the hall, and the bright colours of his shoulder cloth touched the dancing dust with their radiance, transforming the hall into a powerful tableau of sparkling particles and still heads. As the dust started to settle the heads turned more and more in Tankeh's direction. Still he did not move.

The music leaped alive again.

Tankeh raised his head and saw Lemea at the far side of the hall, caught between Masutu and Olembe. His body started jumping, jumping, wanting to dance, refusing to be held back. The sweat was beginning to form, not just in his armpits, but all over, in his hair, on his nose; even the soles of his feet were now meeting the dance floor with a moist touch warmed by the surging blood in him. What was happening to the drums? Where was Benti Edinge? If they delayed in breaking into music he would jump up and dance to the new music in his head. It was there, thumping and rumbling, shaking him and making his head reel.

The hall came alive again. Masutu and Olembe and the other young men standing with them immediately encircled Lemea out of Tankeh Winjala's vision. He shot out his neck and sent a piercing look past the young men, then charged across the dance hall and straight into the circle which he tore into a spectacle of astonished single by-standers.

Benti Edinge caught the glamour in Tankeh Winjala's defiance. As a man to whom music was both trade and medium, but especially medium, Benti Edinge used rhythm to dialogue with the skin and blood, indeed with the life force, of those he played to. Tankeh Winjala standing there in the near end of the hall with Lemea enthralled before him accorded the moment for the intimate intercourse of sound and mood. The rhythms climbed, swelling in volume. Tankeh Winjala fixed his cloth firmly across his shoulder and broke into dance. First he bent and lurched, lurched round and round Lemea, like a cock on heat. Then he pulled back, some distance off, scoured the ground, searched the hall, then broke in Lemea's direction.

She stood torn between admiration and a desire to run off into the darkness outside. She did not yield to the latter urge but stood watching Tankeh as if captivated by the strength that surged from his muscles. Her body trembled, and the eagerness to dance burnt under her skin.

Masutu stormed forward and elbowed Tankeh Winjala violently to the ground and he remained sprawled on the floor in what looked like endless moons of stupor. Then…before Masutu had time to step clear, a sudden flying tackle hit him in the neck. No-one knew when Tankeh rose from the ground into the air. Masutu fell to the ground with the crashing sound of a felled tree. Olembe who had erected himself in front of Lemea bent over and tried to lift Masutu to his feet but the attempt was too heavy for him alone.

With his dusted cloth flipped back into place, Tankeh looked over Olembe's shoulders at Lemea, then broke a path in the crowd of dancers-turned-spectators, and stormed out through the opposite door. Lemea too ran out into the thick night. Olembe ran after her and called into the night but only the echo of his vain voice returned to him.

Chapter Thirteen

We feared for Masutu's life. It was not unusual for anyone who got into a fight with Tankeh Winjala to end up in the grave. So far only I alone had stood up to him. So the fear was deep in people. Those of us present at the dance recalled how Masutu went up like a feather in the wind and came back down with the weight of wet garri paste. I was surprised that he rose at all after that. To see him on his feet was still a wonder happening. As the days passed, the fear increased.

But the fear about Masutu's life was eaten up by an even bigger one: no-one had seen Lemea since the day she disappeared into the dark night. It was just as if she had never existed at all — so thorough were the traces of her absence.

All the powers of the village had been enlisted. Reinforcement had even been sought from Tazim and Fetet. The Council of Chiefs grouping all the paramount authorities of the known tribes had resolved that each ruler dispatch his biggest seer to Nwemba for the search. This had been done and all the seers had seen had been nothing but Lemea's absence.

Mother had grieved and stopped. She did not kill herself as the village feared. She just sat at her door singing songs of loneliness, songs of loss. But seeing the rate at which sorrow was eating her, it would not be long before she slept and did not wake again.

Uncle Abua and I shared waking her up: he would come today and shake her out of sleep, and tomorrow it would be my turn.

129

He for one did not put Lemea's disappearance past Tankeh Winjala. And his conviction was strengthened by the sorrow now hastening his brother's widow to her death.

Tankeh, bringer of sorrow. If you wanted sunshine to run away, bring Tankeh; bring Tankeh to a feast and the meat turned into bones. As one of the survivors who took part in the naming, my uncle had the details in his palms; and as Lemea's absence lasted, memories of Tankeh's birth came more and more alive, and he could not suppress the troubling similarity between the two moments.

In particular, he saw an interesting parallel between the emptiness left by Lemea's disappearance and the terrible void created by the moon of the mudfish, the moon Satmia, Ikom Winjala's wife, was to deliver. "A great drought descended on Nwemba," he recalled, "a great drought that reminded us of what Ikom had gone through in his struggle to raise a big family. Year after year for eight years his wife was pregnant. Year after year for eight years he buried a child. The year Satmia took in this boy called Tankeh, everyone expected her to deliver another victim for the graves. For many days the sun sat straight and tight overhead, chasing away the rainclouds and burning all the bushes into a vast sight of yellow leaves. For the first time Mantum revealed its nakedness, which many villagers ran away from for fear of the fury of the disgraced river spirits. But as the days went by curiosity had the better of their fears and one by one they tiptoed to the edge of the sunken river where first with the corner of their eyes, then with their full eyes, they saw mudfish jumping and tumbling like children in the rain.

"A few intrepid ones ventured onto the bed in the part nearest the bank and seized mudfish with their naked hands. The river gods remained silent. A day passed, two, many, and no god spoke. The young men had discovered a new trade. They scooped up mudfish from the riverbed with their naked hands. This they did for one full moon, in the abandoned hilarity of the dry season sun.

"Then gently, the rainclouds started to gather over the hills of Meamba. The young men took notice, but decided to take home one final catch before the river sprang to life with the return of the rains.

"All that Nwemba counted as young men gathered on the riverbed on the last day to dig up mudfish with their naked hands. Who shall I name and who shall I leave out? All of them. It was as if the village used a broom to sweep all its young men into the riverbed. All day long they dug and scooped to chants and exchange of spicy jokes. They dug and scooped and sang, and did not hear the coming storm. It broke into view suddenly, without any fore-warning, descending in gigantic torrents from the hills of Meamba where it had built up in two days of continuous downpour. It was a magnificent sight. All the young men were swept downstream and over the great waterfall just a short distance below.

"A terrible silence fell on Nwemba. Our old men died and rotted in their houses. Young girls and newly-married women sat at the door and sang sorrowfully to themselves. The seeds…no young men to water them.

"It was in this moon that Ikom Winjala's wife delivered. Hers being the first male child after the calamity of the mudfish, we the ones left behind decided to name him Tankeh: the one who brings sorrow."

Uncle Abua was adamant in his belief. How could a girl disappear into the night as if she was vapour rising from the Mantum falls? He did not attend the dance, but those who did told of how, immediately upon Tankeh's entry into the hall, an unusual sensation had gripped the air and remained there even after his stormy exit.

"The son of Winjala the Crude wants to bring sorrow into my life," he mumbled on his way to see Chief Ndelu. "Let me see what the Chief thinks of this. He at least can be trusted for catching troubling details."

The glow in her eyes as she stood in the middle of the dance hall, how her body shook and the bangles danced on her long arms, how she vanished into the night: Chief Ndelu recalled all this, and each thing he said strengthened Uncle Abua's belief that Tankeh Winjala knew where Lemea had disappeared to.

"What I cannot explain," the Chief said with a troubled air, "is that Tankeh stormed out first. It would have made more sense to me if she had run out first and he had followed. But now I am at a loss."

"Winjala the Crude must have given all his bad powers to his son. He has charmed my daughter. He attended the dance to put a spell on her."

This accusation did not seem to go down well with the Chief, and he made this clear: "I never knew Ikom Winjala to possess any powers. He was a man with a long throat. That one, yes. Remember he ate all the white man's animals he was given charge over."

"And now his son wants to eat my daughter!"

"Loss of your daughter can rightly put such thoughts in your head. But my own feeling sends me in a different direction. I continue to be worried by what I saw. That evening Tankeh Winjala danced the way I had never seen him dance before. Only a stone would not have admired him."

"What is there in a dance to be admired? Did my daughter go there to dance or to admire? And who?"

"Abua, you and I grew up together. Before I succeeded my father we were friends. We did these things together. A good dancer is a winner. Always. You know it."

"Mbe, this is about my daughter."

"Both of us are saying the same thing. I am just as concerned as you are."

"But you seem to be protecting the son of Winjala the Crude."

"I am not protecting anybody. I am just trying to see the thing clearly. You know, things are not always what they seem. I find it hard to silence my inner convictions."

"Mbe, I will come and hang in this palace if anything happens to my daughter."

"The gods guard you against such bad thoughts."

Uncle Abua marched out of the Palace and incurred a sizeable fine for that. The fine he paid amid bitter protestations against the Chief's open support of Winjala's son. He said he did not understand why the Chief was deepening his sorrow. "I have lost my daughter to evil and I must be fined for it."

Some people sympathized with him, but everybody chided him for storming out of the Palace. The Chief was never wrong, he was reminded.

Chapter Fourteen

The solitary house remained enveloped in mystery. As usual, smoke trickled through the grass roof in the evening; but whereas this had been only an occasional happening in the past, the village was now puzzled at the new pace. White smoke dribbling from the distant roof was now a familiar evening sight so that people had gone into the habit of closing their day with lively comments on it.

"The tongues...they are bigger today..."

"Bigger still than yesterday... he must have built a big fire"

"The wood he carries home. Can that be for him alone?"

"The nearby forests."

"He will soon empty them."

"Only until very recently a log lasted him five sunsets."

"Five, and more, but now the pace has gone up."

"A log per sunset now."

"Strange, strange."

Unlike my sister whom nobody had seen since the night of the dance, Tankeh Winjala had remained a solid part of the village. He crisscrossed it more frequently now than was his habit.

Anyone just newly arrived in Nwemba would have vowed that Tankeh was the busiest in the village; and he would not be wrong.

Judging by the number of times he was seen each day and by the way he burned his energy in village events, he was easily the most active man in all Nwemba. Take the case of Waikum's death. Tankeh washed and dressed the corpse, dug the grave, contributed three calabashes of good wine, sang throughout the two-day vigil, did the propitiatory dance round the corpse, and heaved the corpse into the grave single-handedly when the time came for it.

Surprise caught everybody. Even Sendelenghi who was known to side with him in all circumstances good or bad this time expressed his perplexity openly. "Tankeh has shed his skin," he was heard to be saying. "The new layer he is showing us now seems to come from a different snake."

Tankeh Winjala was actually seen selling game in nearby village markets and buying food items. Yet others had seen him pricing and buying expensive cloth – blue wax print with minute family scenes of mothers in the midst of well-fed children.

The glowing warmth over his house contrasted with the sorrow in Nwemba. For many moons the whereabouts of Lemea had gnawed a big hole in hearts, especially those of the women. No-one had seen her for eight moons, or heard from her; eight long moons during which two harvests had enriched the corn barns.

People had thought of many things…Lemea had hanged herself like Sema who put her neck in a noosed cloth on the day of her wedding…she had fled the village with a young man the way Nina or Minda would do, especially Nina who was known to go freely from one man to the other the way a butterfly danced among petals. But then, as these thoughts came and went, the people remained troubled by the full count of Nwemba's young men. None of them was missing. They were all in their houses, all at their trades. No young man had dropped out of the line like a missing wrestler in a tournament. Even those of them who in the past had hung on the skin of Nwemba like parasites were now in its main bloodstream, not sucking or poisoning it, but filling it with new strength.

Tankeh Winjala for one caught the fancy of the wondering village with his generous burst of activity. One moon to the fishing festival he paid me a visit. I fled into the shrub behind my house on seeing who my visitor was and remained there until the apparition vanished.

He placed a calabash at my door and strode away.

I re-appeared many moments later and then only to hurry the calabash with all its content to Uncle Abua and Aunt Sabina. All kinds of things danced in my head over what Tankeh Winjala had done. Puzzling act, one moon to the festival. What exactly was the son of Winjala up to?

Uncle Abua had to stand outside in the middle of the night and chase away the bad spirits. With Lemea missing for so many moons, with the second contest so near, just one moon away, this was not the kind of visit to fill the head with quiet sleep. The old ones of the family had to put their heads together.

I even thought, why worry the old ones of the family? They had more than enough on their hands, what with their daughter missing for so many moons most of them thought and talked only things of sorrow. I could even just pour the thing outside, somewhere behind my house, and rest the matter there. That way Tankeh Winjala's evil plans would go with the spilled wine. Son of Winjala the Crude, yardman to the white man. Very much like him to think only bad things. Evil ran in their bloodstream the way treacherous waters crashed down the jagged course of Mantum. His father had lived cutting grass and had extended the cutting to the white man's animal friends, the last and most painful one to the white man being his big monkey friend Stirrup. Before Stirrup the white man had lost many others of his animal friends to Winjala's murderous swings – snakes, deer, birds – but no death had pained him like the death of Stirrup.

Thanks to many months of caring attention from its master, Stirrup had jumped in just a matter of weeks from a sickly, death-threatened little monkey into a lively bulk of flesh into which the white man's repeated techniques had put some very arresting reflexes. Stirrup could now walk on hindlegs and greet with his forelegs in alternate gestures. In a special jabber meaningful only to its master, he could relate the day's happenings, reveal poor conduct on the part of attendants, or recommend good treatment whenever such was the case. Quite often, upon returning from a working trip, Harrington would chide Winjala the Crude after Stirrup's report, and the yardman would heap himself near the animal fence and throw threatening looks in the direction of a jubilant Stirrup as it taunted and capered just within annoying reach.

The last time Harrington saw Stirrup alive the unsuspecting white man called my father his washerman to his side to share with him the unique spectacle of a standoff between his little friend and the yardman.

"Stirrup is worked up," he said to his amazed washerman.

"Yes, Sa," my father answered.

"Watch the way he is bobbing."

"Yes Sa."

"He doesn't do that with you."

"Yes Sa."

"There's something about this man Stirrup doesn't like."

"Yes Sa."

"Whatever you people do in my absence he sees, and reports to me when I return."

"We wok popo, Sa," my father said, to which the white man specified:

"You, Seima, yes, surely, but not that one dumped there. He's much worse than my companions he kills."

"Yes Sa," my father answered before being tapped off on the back. As he departed into the more familiar world of his laundry room, Harrington descended into his cane chair and before long the sight of Winjala the Crude heaped against the protective mesh blended with the lively population within into the defining moment of a lifetime's quest…the high school in St. Ives, Cornwall. Michael Dunton, physics teacher and globetrotter...his many trips to Africa...the proud record of enlightenment. Each trip to the continent had cemented his belief in the human race as one indivisible reality, which the last ten minutes of his Thursday classes had been dedicated to sinking into his pupils. Chalk flipped aside and one buttock on the classroom table, he uttered the appeal with Christian fidelity:

"Your life must be fired by a grand ideal. And there is no greater one than bringing down the artificial frontiers between men. You will not understand me sitting here. You need to travel out, to the places on earth where the semblance of difference stands like a threat to the truth of oneness. England gives you only part of the truth about the human race. The other part, and an even greater part, lies in the continents beyond, in those places you hear about only when suffering is on the table. Suffering is part of the truth, but not all of it. There is also joy in those places, joy of the kind you experience when you play football on a muddy pitch and tumble on each other."

The absence of drama in his teacher's presentation of distant realities captured Harrington's imagination and dragged him forever more deeply into the fantasy of this world that lay beyond but that was not different from a football pitch in which players tumbled on each other in mirthful abandon.

A degree in zoology and just enough time to honeymoon with Lucy before answering the invitation from the Overseas Office to travel to the Atlantic Ocean village of Ediki-Mbeng on the West African coast for purposes first of linking it up to Meamba further inland., then of identifying and classifying all the bird species in the area.

Among his equipment was a mental gear that Dunton had warned all prospective travellers not to leave behind: the readiness to expect not only logic but the surprising. Although he emphasised oneness over difference, he conceded to there being moments, happenings, events, that stretched the faith in oneness to breaking point. These instances he called the surprising...you will meet many surprises, but you must accommodate them. On no account must they dig in. If they do, if you allow them to, stereotypes will defeat your sunrays. Your logic must cushion the surprising, not magnify it. You will look at the human race the way you look at the human body, with different parts doing different things. If you do so, you will not expect one part to perform the functions of another part, and you will know that without one the other will be dead, whichever way you take it.

Chapter Fifteen

Uncle Abua loved palmwine, best of all when it touched the tongue with a flavour of intrigue. He had the mouth of a connoisseur and could tell good palmwine with a drop against his tongue. Knowledge of the thing had settled in layers in him like dregs at the bottom of a calabash. And yet for all his familiarity with the stuff he remained above its influence, helped in this by the sampler's rather than the drinker's attitude with which he related to the stuff. He always credited palmwine with powers to reveal hidden meanings, unspoken designs; so even when he drank, it was more to sharpen his awareness than to lose himself.

Tankeh Winjala was not among his best-loved names; and this was the least that could be said. For one thing, he could never bring himself to understand why a young man would elect to throw himself out of the run of communal life when there was so much more to gain by being in the thick of it. The distant sight of Tankeh's house perched in solitary defiance on the spot of the old village shrine always caused considerable irritation to swell in him.

"Look at all that expanse of land," he would cry out, sweeping the vast divide with his trembling stretched-out hand. "Why not build closer, even somewhere in between?"

These interrogations had taken on more intensity recently, what with the exile's increasing participation in village life there had been a general feeling that he wanted to cut the rope of isolation. My arrival with palmwine purported to have been brought to me by Tankeh Winjala therefore filled Uncle Abua with both amusement and excitement.

As for Aunt Sabina, the whole story accompanying the palmwine sounded too unexpected to be taken at face value. Even in Tazim where she led a quiet married life, people knew of Tankeh Winjala and his queer ways…the unresolved death of girls, our recent fight, these were the sort of things to expect from him, not him visiting his sworn rival in broad daylight with palmwine. Who in his right senses would believe such a thing?

"This your Tankeh Winjala, is he a different one from the son of Winjala the Crude?" In making this inquiry she knew that the authentic son of Winjala the Crude would not betray the lineage code of hatred which he as the last survivor had the duty to protect and project.

"The same one. He did not come at night for me to say I did not see him well."

"I do not know what's in all this," Uncle Abua said, "but I believe what Banda is saying. If there's anybody in this village who knows Tankeh Winjala, he is that person."

"Believing him is one thing. But what is in this palmwine? That's what I want to know," Aunt Sabina said. "Where is Lemea? I should have prepared her long ago and returned to my farms. But here I am. What is in this wine? You people should tell me."

"Whatever is in it, I will drink it," Uncle Abua said, almost triumphantly. "I have tasted it and it sits well on my tongue."

"Not this wine," I protested.

Aunt Sabina shot to her feet and seized the calabash by the neck.

"It shall be drunk. My brother and I will drink it. Wait. The smoked caterpillars. That was the last thing Lemea brought here before disappearing. I'll steam some in oil and prepare some foo-foo to go with."

"Listen, my son," Uncle Abua trumpeted, "in life when you offer your hand to evil it crushes it. Use your hand to crush evil, to defeat it. My sister and I will drink this palmwine. Whatever the reason Tankeh brought it, we will put our own reason into it. Your aunt will prepare foo-foo corn…hot…and steam the caterpillars in oil that trickles between the fingers."

"And all of us will eat," Aunt Sabina concurred from near the fireplace where the caterpillars were sizzling.

"I will not eat the food or drink the palmwine," I said with stubbornness that Uncle Abua found to be out of place, but which he did nothing to challenge.

"I won't even encourage you to taste of any," Aunt Sabina said. "Lemea said she did not know where the caterpillars were from. Your Uncle and I can eat that kind of thing; but not you. At least you know who brought the palmwine, and I agree that you should not drink it. My brother and I can die, but you must live on to win the next fishing contest and find and bring back Lemea."

"There's nothing in this calabash to kill anyone," Uncle Abua said in challenge. "You want to see?" At this he poured a cowhornfull and sent it down in one uninterrupted gulp before saying in my direction: "You did well to bring the calabash here."

"He did well," Aunt Sabina concurred.

Uncle Abua reached for the calabash and jumped out into the descending night. Aunt Sabina seized me by the hand and pulled me outside and we all stood facing the stars. After a brief but enchanting moment of communion with the unseen, Aunt and Uncle returned into the house and settled on the foo-foo with caterpillars steamed in palmoil.

All this happened without me. I had walked off in the night with nothing on my tongue.

Chapter Sixteen

I walked off, not home, but to see Masutu in bed, neck swollen where the flying charge had hit him. The swelling was caught in ghelang paste.

"This is me," Masutu said with considerable effort, touching the swelling lightly.

"At least your head did not fall off," I returned in sympathy.

"The bad thing about it," he struggled, "the really bad thing…"

I stopped him: "Don't worsen your condition. I will return tomorrow."

"No," he shouted abruptly as he lifted himself up from the bed. "Don't go yet. This pain is not my worst torment."

I brought myself back from the door as if his words had transformed into orders I could not resist. Returning into the house was like journeying into the heart of a new revelation. The energy with which he lifted himself up from the bed was not commonplace: some underlying force must have borne him upwards, lifted him body and mind, and placed those resolute words in his mouth. The words sounded musical and ominous, strong and enchanting, all at the same time. His face too, from the creased contortions of pain, had transformed, almost instantaneously, into a smooth appearance to which pain was as foreign as tears to laughter.

He sat up in bed propped against his left hand and the right flung menacingly outwards, then began, pointing to a sight visible only to him alone: "He stepped into this house."

I listened and looked, following the threatening hand where it pointed, but saw nothing.

"Tankeh Winjala," he said. Once the name leapt from his lips he fell back in bed as if delivered of a burden that had sat on his chest and pressed him down. Even his breathing changed and a new peace lit his face.

I stared, aghast, then said both in surprise and confusion: "So he did."

"With a calabash of wine. And sat himself there…there," he cried, pointing at a distant stool. "Then he said he was sorry. Actually said that…to me. I've not ceased to wonder."

I listened to all this with a peculiar feeling of familiarity, of teasing repetition. Should I reveal my own side of the story? The startling coincidences fed the urge in me to it, but somehow I reined in the pressure. I needed to eat and digest the meaning in what was unfolding. One man could not put our judgment to so much test, unless he had a new resolve to turn us and our reasoning into big fools. The saying went that a snake did not break new paths everyday but followed its beaten trail, day after day. Snake-hunters recited this habit as the key to the standoff between the reptile and them, and said there was no more dangerous twist than when a path was abandoned for a new one: each new opened path was a new danger for the hunter, each abandoned trail new trap for the trapper. Once a snake shed its skin it never returned to the spot of the happening, unless to strike down the unwary hunter who mistook the shed skin for the living reptile.

I could not say why exactly, but there seemed to be something in the happenings of the recent days that brought to mind the sly ruses of a snake. Tankeh Winjala had become intractable, unknowable. He no longer came when everyone looked down the road; no longer cut a gash in confirmation of fears. His image had blurred a lot, so that now it was no longer possible to say precisely just who one was dealing with when it came to him: the son of Winjala the Crude, keeper of the anti-Harrington oath, or a new man who saw in palmwine the cementing power of friendship. It was no longer possible.

I noticed that Masutu still had things in his belly to voice out, so I extended my stay in the hope that some of those things would hasten my understanding of the other troubling revelations already sitting in my head.

"Lemea," Masutu resumed, "any news?"

"Nothing that I can hang on."

"We are talking about my future wife. This neck…I would have brought her back."

"You talk of the future. And the present? What am I without my sister?"

"The future and now are just one. But what do I call this? Escape or what?"

"Escape? And with whom? Lemea would not run away with anyone outside you. She'd told me so."

"I believe that, but with women you can never tell."

"Kidnapping?"

"Nobody carried her out of the dancehall. She ran out on her own feet. The whole trouble is there."

"Deep trouble," I repeated.

I rose to leave but Masutu waved me back onto the stool.

"One broomstick cannot be stronger than the bundle," he said half in confidence, half in caution.

"Never," I returned even though I did not know why he called up such wisdom.

"Take it home," he said, waving and watching me go.

The darkness outside was more of an evening darkness than the darkness of night. It was not lost in the menacing silence of late hours, nor in the eerie hoots and rippling roars of totemic birds and animals. In temper it fell among those evenings set aside for visits and gossips, especially for dance and courtship. I felt like everything except going home.

Home. And mother's repeated talk of wife and children. She never said wives. I laughed at the care she took when talking about that side of things. Wife. Not wives. Not a first wife to begin with. So all left to her…

And where did I place Nina? She called herself my mother; that she had delivered me a second time. Which was true. She had brought me to this life again, shown me the deeper truths in things. So where did I put her in this dance of wife and children? Nowhere, really. That was easy to say. Everywhere was nowhere. I could not beat my chest in the midst of stains. And there were many of them. The evening I came when she was not expecting me and found the door locked and the house shaking at its foundations, I waited outside until the house stopped shaking, then she came out and lied to me that she was alone in the house, only for Sendelenghi to come out with her cloth round his waist to ask me what I was looking for and whether I was not ashamed to stand in front of a locked door like a ngong dog in front of a pot of soup. I could have seized him by that cloth and exposed his wrinkled thing to the shame of the disappearing sun. I did not do that. I only laughed and walked away.

With thoughts like that and many more in my mind about Nina I could not give her a place in my search for a wife. After your mother, a wife was the next dearest person. In certain ways she was even the dearest. You did not choose your mother; but you chose your wife. The affection you had for your mother was founded on duty and tradition. But the one you had for the woman you chose was of a different kind. It was not dictated by the people around you but by the desires in you; desire for safety, desire for confidence, desire for happiness. Anything that faulted any one of these desires also drove away the marriage dream. That is why I could not consider Nina for marriage. She was alright when it came to doing certain things with her, things she also did with other people, like Sendelenghi; but when the matter of marriage was under consideration, she disappeared from the scene.

Yeisi. Yeisi. I could hear the proud ripples. They came back to me clearly, as if they knew where they belonged.

Wife and children.

If the preparations went fast, Aunt Sabina could receive her into the family and teach her a few things before returning to Tazim. For one thing, her coming would bring some shine into mother's brooding. She had good ways. Mother herself had said so; had said daughter resembled mother.

Now that I was marching home, who was I to meet there? Who was to welcome me with a concerned frown? I could change my mind and go instead to…to where? I wanted to spread myself somewhere and be touched, pressed. I had forgotten my body for so long! Even now, in the quiet breeze of night, I could hear it protesting under my skin. Body and its things. Nina. Ninaaa! The bad side of man. Could she hear me? Could she feel the revolt in my body? The heat?

In moments of this kind when it was the body calling, commanding, you reached into the bag of acts gone and pulled out one that guided your response. I refuse to yield this time. If I search I will pull out one that shows me with Nina. And the blood will run again faster, hotter. I will not. Instead, I will tie the mouth of the bag tight and fling it far, far into the dark night so that it falls beyond my reach for always.

Chapter Seventeen

Masutu improved fast, thanks mainly to the ghelang paste and its work on the damaged parts of his neck, especially the flesh underneath. You had to look at him closely to know that Tankeh's flying leg had nearly split his neck into two; and even looking at him closely still did not give any trace away of something bad having happened. The healing was thorough; so much so that he was ready to carry logs of wood to prove his regained fitness.

Now that he was back on his feet and the swelling in his neck something of the past, I could go ahead with my marriage plans. He had been one of the reasons why I had held them back.

Not he alone.

Lemea too.

For many nights I had lain with my eyes wide open searching my ceiling for where she could have disappeared to. What would my marriage be like without her? Who would fill the air with wililis? Who would sit by my new woman on her first evening in my house? Who would serenade her into my bed? Her first warm bath as a wife – who would prepare it?

My mind went back to Meamba, to the time when we were growing up there with my father as washerman to the white man Harrington. Lemea had grown up sealed away from the wider society. My father always said her own school was by her mother, where she was supposed to learn the basic things of the home. But there were many things he did not know about his daughter: that she admired pictures in the books I brought back from school; that she had stood up to Njitifuh at the playgrounds. If he had examined his mind well enough, he would have stumbled on that day when she questioned him about the difference between the things the white woman wore closest to her skin and those the white man wore. I had not forgotten those questions; not even our mother had. She had shown anger at what she thought was impudence on her daughter's part: "You don't ask your father that kind of question." And in reply Lemea had said they were just conversing. But the whole thing went beyond just conversing. Her question to our father in a matter in which he felt so much pain showed clearly that she did not see things in the same way as he saw them. Just when he was losing sweat at the mere thought of washing the things a woman wore closest to her body, his own daughter threw it in his face that she did not see any difference between what a man wore closest to his skin and what a woman wore closest to her skin.

It was this same Lemea that stood her ground before Njitifuh when all the other girls of her age group were too terrified to even hang around when the young tyrant approached. A girl capable of such acts was capable of any act. Now she had stormed out of a dance in the village. With her there was never any warning sign. My father did not expect the question she asked him. Njitifuh never expected her in his path. The night she disappeared from the dance hall there was no forerunning sign that any storm was gathering. Where could one search for such a character? If Yeisi did that anyone in the village would know where to go and be sure to find her in the second or third house. It would not go beyond that. If Nina did such a thing people would first laugh, then go straight to where she was and bring her back home. In all her disorder she was that predictable. But with Lemea, where did one start?

It was not even the marriage as such that made her absence so hard to bear. Just the fact of her not being there was enough to turn my day into night. It was not as if she had died and we had buried her in a specific place that I could go to and talk to her from this side; or as if she was lying somewhere the way Masutu lay for many moons with the flesh in his neck kicked into a lump by Tankeh. Nothing of the sort. There were just two of us, not like in other families where there were enough children to build a wrestling team. With her gone I was amputated, reduced to a half person. Her absence reminded me of the way I felt each time I thought of the white man; of how he had everything and I had nothing. Lemea was not only my sister: she was my conscience. She was younger than me in age but far older than me in courage; in determination. When she set her mind to something it stayed on that something until it was done. She did not know fear, unless of things that made her small.

Could I count on the marriage for some good luck? If Lemea was alive and heard that I was marrying, she would certainly come out of her hiding and be part of the celebration. I was certain. She could not hear that I was marrying and not be part of it; not with her warnings full of laughter: "I'm your sister, not your wife. Marry quick and let some of this trouble fall from my back." And then when the thing was about to happen she allowed herself to be swallowed by silence. It was thanks to her that Yeisi said yes. Yeisi with whom she got along so well. Everyone was agreed that they were more of sisters than friends, and each time she had the chance to, she told me how happy she would be the day Yeisi was escorted to my house.

"And you," I would challenge, "whose palmwine will you want us to drink?"

She wouldn't answer immediately but would return to my own marriage with Yeisi: "Don't mind about me. Let Yeisi come first."

"Were you not happy the day she said Olembe and his people could drink Uncle Abua's palmwine?"

"An evening has never been softer on my skin."

153

"Or did you want my uncle to be driven away with his palmwine?"

"The gods forbid."

"So tell me."

Each time I got to this last point she tactfully surrendered the matter to Uncle Abua and Aunt Sabina who to her had the last say. Their choice was Dinga, a stout young man, but a young man for whom Lemea had only disdain. Whenever she pronounced his name she held her mouth as if she had tasted food without salt. She called his name again, with all the signs of distance that her lips could say.

"That's for Uncle Abua and Aunt Sabina. Yours. It is your own I want. I should know whose palmwine I'm washing my cowhorn for."

"In that case don't wash it at all."

I knew how hard it was for a girl to say where her eyes went, so this in and out of the bush game did not worry me that much. Besides, Lemea was no girl not to speak her mind when the occasion demanded it. When the time came for it, she would certainly tell all of us to our faces what she was thinking.

As the marriage day came closer I slept with my door and my eyes wide open and jumped at the smallest sound. When a rat crossed the floor I jumped; when the wind moved my door I jumped even faster. Lemea was in every little thing that agitated the growing silence in my life.

Then I said I had to be a man and go ahead with the marriage.

I did, and soon Yeisi was in my house.

Oh, when I say soon it is as if I just went to visit and returned with her. Nothing of the sort. Even Olembe surprised me; Olembe who had given me all the promises and encouragement. I knew that all left to him, I could come for Yeisi any day. It was not going to be like that. He turned round and showed me amba. For two weeks I could not see Yeisi; for two weeks I could not hear her voice. Uncle Abua went there and came back. Olembe refused even to let him enter his house. I sent Minda thinking that Olembe would be softer with her. He was instead harder. He turned her away before she got near the house. She came back covered in shame and fright. Uncle Abua said enough was enough, that he would arrange a different marriage for me; that Olembe could carve a man for his sister but that that man was no longer going to be me. My mother said the time had come for her to die. She had only stayed alive because she wanted to carry my child in her arms before dying, but now that Olembe had stood in the way of that happiness, she was going to die, that she had already lost her daughter and now was not going to see the grandchildren she had put all her hopes on. The confusion was total, the disappointment deep.

Then one night Yeisi jumped into my house and hid behind the door. That same night I sneaked her to Uncle Abua and early at daybreak I marched to Olembe to ask for my wife. It was only then that he discovered that the cage was empty. He laughed and we shook hands for long in the middle of the compound.

Soon she started vomiting everything she ate, and asking for palmwine early in the morning only to start vomiting again at the mere sight of it. Aunt Sabina who had since returned to Tazim came back and took her away, leaving me once again alone. But the loneliness this time was different. I saw it in my mother's eyes. She said death could now wait; that she had found a new reason to live on for a few more moons.

The reason soon became two reasons. Lemea entered the house early one morning carrying a child on her back. She untied the child, a big boy with sharp eyes, and placed him in her mother's trembling hands, just long enough for her mother to dot the child's forehead with two drops of grateful tears. Then she took the child back and went towards the door, saying at the threshold:

"Mother, I will return after the fishing contest to tell you where I am."

Chapter Eighteen

Dry season came, and with it the second contest. All the nets were out, and the village was also humming with names of the favourite contenders…Banda…Tankeh. Where two people stood, only our two names were mentioned. It was as if all other names in Nwemba had merged into our own. We had each won the contest once before. That in itself was enough reason to put fire to the appetite for this one. But that was not the main reason why the village was caught in a kind of contest fever. The things our two parents had said on dying kept the contest alive; tipped it out of its usual frame. Winjala the Crude had said that he did not want the white man's ways in Nwemba; Sama Gakoh that he wanted them. And it was the contest to decide.

Tankeh's name kept on coming even though no-one had seen his net. Those who called his name said the year he won no-one saw his net before the contest, yet he won. This time too that no-one was seeing his net, why should he not win again? His supporters seemed driven by an inner faith in him made all the stronger by his past feat. Once a winner, always a winner, they seemed to be saying. And they did not go and hide behind the house to voice their feelings. They filled the village with their optimism, led in the charge by Sendelenghi. He was anything but subdued in asserting that Tankeh would claim the contest. Even if he had consulted with the spirits of Mantum and been handed the verdict, he would not have spoken with more assurance.

Others pinned their choice on me, but with less certainty. I too had won the contest once before, but there was no young man ready to drown the village in my prowess the way Sendelenghi was doing for Tankeh. Masutu could have done it. He even tried, but Sendelenghi was just too much for him.

Sendelenghi – he had a way of shouting you to silence that made any verbal tussle with him very frustrating. Because he was tall and lanky, even when he was looking at you ordinarily, you kept feeling the oppressive weight of his head on your own as if he had given it to you to carry. And then you wanted to tell him to stop doing that, only to see that the more you told him not to look down on you because you were no servant of his, the more he transferred the arrogance to his voice and used it to cower you. With him on Tankeh's side, it was difficult to see how victory would escape them. The only fear about the contest was the way the gods could decide at times. You could come filled with confidence in your luck, then throw your net and haul little stones and other tiny objects. And someone else standing by you so that if you moved your toes just a bit you could touch his own and who threw his own net with no hope would need eight other hands to help him drag his catch. The gods were like that. But if it were all just a matter of who talked loudest and longest, there was no doubt about where victory would go in any contest in Nwemba.

One week to the contest, part of Ndelu's priests moved their ritual hut to the banks of Mantum to be within earshot of the gods. It was important for them to do so: the gods could speak words of meaning to the village and there would be no ear to catch what they said, as it happened the year Fofang won the contest for the first time. A voice rose from the undercurrents of Mantum, heavy with anguish. First it licked the steep edges of the bank on the side of Nwemba, climbing like one with a heavy burden on his back, climbed until it reached the forlorn shore where it remained for many days waiting for human ears to take back its message to the village. No-one came, so it fell back into the depths leaving only an eerie ripple of sounds to roll on the grass in the direction of the village. Many old men caught the ripple and shuddered at the threatening emptiness of the noise. They knew voices from the deep never left emptiness in their wake but one calamity or the other. It was not long before the women went to the farm and came back as they went. The cornfields had turned yellow, from lush green, and were all bent to one side, sleeping, as if caressed by a bad wind.

When the gods were angry, they sent a dry, crackling sound into the village with nothing in it but whizzing and whistling. And shortly afterwards calamity struck.

This time the priests made sure the voice from the deeps did not come and go back with its message. Already, the two prize goats had been chosen from the palace herd and tied apart in a stretch of green grass where they fed daily, raising their heads now and again from the grass to look at Benti and Sani Edinge as they rehearsed the victory dance.

Only Tankeh's net was not seen. Otherwise the village was a sight of coloured weaves in different shapes and sizes fluttering in the wind.

Talk had gone from Nwemba through Tazim to Fetet about the contest and what it held for the village. This was not the first contest of its kind. Only that it was the one each person wanted to witness; to see with his own eyes so that he too would say I saw it, not that I was told…I was there.

It was like the birth of a new child. Those who witnessed the happening, who waited in the male house round a calabash and caught the first distant cries of the new child from the women's house, those ones talked differently, talked with pride and the certainty of an eye witness. They were the first to know whether it was man or woman; first to give it a name.

People came to Nwemba to see it happen. They came in such numbers that there was no empty space on the banks on the day itself.

Early in the morning of the contest we all fell into the river at the gong, sending up a big splash. Each person fell into his own chosen spot and worked his net only there.

The dry season flow was without the power and rush of the rainy season torrents, but it was still strong enough to sweep you downstream if you left your feet dancing, as it had happened a few times in the past, bringing the contest to a mournful halt.

Everybody wedged their feet against a stone which they knew to be heady to the tides, then flung their nets wide, talking to them, praising them, urging them on.

Soon I felt my net pull away as if tugged by an opposing force. I dug my heels into the bed and dragged. The net was heavier than even in the year I won the contest. I threw it out on the bank first, then jumped out after it. The crowd was not mistaken. Although I was not the first to jump out, they knew that from the way they were seeing my net, the contest was as good as over. They broke into celebration.

Everybody danced where they were standing, and turned to catch the hands of their neighbours. But not Chief Ndelu. He remained unaffected. Ordinarily, he would have raised his hand and given the signal for the start of celebration. This time he did not. He just sat on his royal stool and watched his people as if he was not part of what they were seeing. Without him taking part, the people looked rather foolish in their celebration. He allowed them to go on like that for some time, then he rose to his feet and waved for silence, and sat back down.

The loud noises died into surprised murmurs.

"The Chief is not seeing like us."

"Nothing bigger can come out of Mantum."

"See what the others are throwing out."

"And Tankeh, what is he still doing in the river?"

"Shame." The one who said this raised his voice just a bit too high and the insult in it reached Sendelenghi's ears.

"Who talks of shame? You Masutu?" he shot back, marching forward in the same breath.

"Me," said the author of the first word. "Is it a lie?"

"We will soon know who is shamed, you big-mouthed fool. The winning fish is still coming, but you stand there like a bent tree and talk about shame."

"As usual you think it's talk that catches fish," Masutu fought back boldly, refusing this time to concede any ground to Sendelenghi.

"Shame, truly. He knows Banda has won," another young man standing by Masutu ventured.

"You just sow up your ugly lips," Sendelenghi bellowed, and the young man fell silent.

"Let us wait and see," Masutu said, in a sign of appeasement.

"Let us wait and see. See what?" Sendelenghi questioned, even though Tankeh's prolonged stay in the river was beginning to worry him.

"Soon the gong will go," Masutu blew out in half triumph.

"And the Chief will declare Banda the winner," the young man by him rounded up. Sendelenghi moved away, as if to leave them to their delusions.

"See the goats," Masutu said.

"Yes, see the way they are looking at Banda. Even they already know their new owner." The other young man added.

"Let the gong go quick so that the music can start. My limbs want to dance," Masutu said almost impatiently.

As they talked like that their eyes were on the bank of Mantum, the Nwemba side, searching it with anxious eyes. Most contestants had climbed out by now with their catch. Only Tankeh was still awaited. Very unusual. This was the third contest he was entering. In the first he had emerged first from the river. But he had not won that season. In the second four other people had come out before him. And he had won. What was happening now did not resemble anything he had accustomed them to. With him still in the river, it was as if the contest was still ahead too; as if what they were seeing was not the real thing but a rehearsal. All the same they danced, some half-heartedly, some not at all.

Those who had pinned their hopes on Tankeh were the most disturbed. Some of them went up and down the bank nervously. Sendelenghi for one folded his arms behind his back and marched up and down, going so near the bank edge at times that it was feared he would miss a step and end up in the river.

Only the ritual injunction stopped him from searching the river for Tankeh. If he looked into it before the victory gong went, he would be sent away immediately and banned from the next three contests. So he did not look into the river despite the swollen eagerness in him to do so. Many others like him held themselves together, making what business they could of the agitation in them.

Almost every contestant had by now come out to the bank. The different catches panted and skipped on the grass, drawing comments of admiration from the spectators, but also whispers of surprise, especially of worry.

Just then shouts like thunder surged from the watching throats. Tankeh had just thrown his net on the bank with fish that no-one had ever seen and for which the village had no name. The bank broke into dance and wilililis.

Sendelenghi pushed forward and raced to the bank and lifted Tankeh to his shoulders and circled him round the open space, then settled him before Chief Ndelu who had descended back into his seat even as the rest of the crowd kept on dancing.

Masutu and Olembe tried to raise me to their shoulders too but gave up the idea when they caught Sendelenghi in one of his derisive laughs.

Two of the priests stepped forward and emptied all the catches in the open space. Then one by one they placed them in a line according to sizes, each fish by its net.

No word was spoken.

No sound was made.

At the end Tankeh's fish was put at the head of the line, then my own.

Now that the catches were laid out on the ground, it looked as if there was not much difference between Tankeh's fish and my own. The people seemed to have shouted more out of relief at seeing Tankeh emerge than out of admiration for his catch. It even took the priests some time to decide which one to place at the head of the line. First they put mine, stepped behind, looked at the two, then came back and changed their places.

Although Tankeh's fish topped the line, he did not throw out his hands in victory. He stood before the Chief as if he was not the one who caught the winning fish. Again everyone went into murmurs of wonder:

"Does he know he has won?"

"What has become of his proud tongue?"

"Tankeh is a changed man."

"He is not even dancing."

"He will kill the celebration."

Even I was surprised at Tankeh's detachment, especially when I thought of what the victory meant for him and for the wish his father had left behind. He could not have worked so hard for the victory only to spit on it when it finally came. What had he spent many nights by the bank for? Was it not for this moment? Why had he invoked my name for weeks running and challenged me to fights time without number if not for this moment? Where was this borrowed humility from? And yet when one looked at him one saw that he was not pretending, that there was no joy in him at his achievement. It even looked as though he would not hesitate to throw his catch back into the river if he was asked to do so.

The First Priest sent Tankeh to the centre where he stood facing the chief. The place went silent. Any time the gong would go and Chief Ndelu would declare Tankeh the winner.

The crowd listened and looked. The gong-beater especially was waiting for the sign from the chief for him to give a peel of the liberating sounds. But instead of ordering the gong to go, the chief rose and paced towards the bank of Mantum, towards the point where the water disappeared into a fall. The priests followed, but he waved them back and continued alone. He paced on until he was lost in the rising vapours of the fall.

There was a good sun overhead, and it spread its rays softly for the season.

Tankeh remained at the centre, looking past the crowd. Something said I should rush to him and hold his hand and say well done, but I did not do it since I wondered how he would take it. I could rush to him and he would enter my legs and throw me to the ground, so unpredictable was he. So I left him alone and instead searched the crowd for Olembe's eyes. It was as if he too was eager for our eyes to meet because they did so almost instantly. I knew when his eyes were alive and when they were not. This time they were. They seemed to tell me something beyond the contest, something that had brought a big change to his way of seeing and reasoning. He ran his two hands over his stomach, then made the sign of two: delivery... two. Could it be that Manyi had delivered two kids? I looked at Olembe again and he confirmed my thinking, then took his eyes away from me almost immediately, as though to say that was all he had for me.

My eyes remained where they had met Olembe's, but in the place of his eyes now stood those of a mother-goat and two kids. Manyi licking her kids clean. Would they be allowed to live? That question shook me and forced my look towards the line the priests had drawn on the ground with our different catches, and in which my fish was not the winning fish.

164

The chief returned from the bank and strode straight back to his seat. My eyes danced between him and the line of fish on the ground...Manyi... the threat of exile. Could this be my last day in Nwemba? Manyi. And Manyi? Had she given birth only to die again? I looked at the crowd and saw that everyone was looking at me. They had caught the meaning in the moment. Tankeh had won. His victory would soon be proclaimed, and a lifetime of exile pronounced on me. I swallowed hot saliva and it descended into my stomach to meet a burning question addressed to my father. Had I not done my duty by him? Where was he at this particular instant? "Father, where are you?" I mumbled.

Just then Chief Ndelu rose to his feet and ordered that I too be sent to join Tankeh where he was standing. A big shudder of amazement gripped the crowd. They were watching what they had never seen before. As soon as I joined Tankeh in the opening, the chief ordered that the fatter goat be handed to Tankeh and the smaller one to me. At this a tremulous wililili tore the air. I turned to see Lemea with one hand to her mouth and the other pressing a child to her side. She did not wait again for more words from Chief Ndelu but carried her child off to tell mother where she was.